Mack Dunstan's

Inferno

Paul Collins

iUniverse, Inc.
Bloomington

Mack Dunstan's Inferno

The views expressed in this work are solely those of the author and do not necessarily reflect the views of the publisher, and the publisher hereby disclaims any responsibility for them.

iUniverse books may be ordered through booksellers or by contacting:

iUniverse
1663 Liberty Drive
Bloomington, IN 47403
www.iuniverse.com
1-800-Authors (1-800-288-4677)

Because of the dynamic nature of the Internet, any web addresses or links contained in this book may have changed since publication and may no longer be valid.

Any people depicted in stock imagery provided by Thinkstock are models, and such images are being used for illustrative purposes only.
Certain stock imagery © Thinkstock.

ISBN: 978-1-4620-3276-1 (sc)
ISBN: 978-1-4620-3280-8 (ebk)

Printed in the United States of America

iUniverse rev. date: 04/13/2012

Mack Dunstan's
Inferno

CHAPTER ONE

"I think I'll just take a nap," he exclaimed to the doctor and nurse, as they took his temperature.

Lines now crossed his face, which had thinned. Silver hair adorned his head. The twinkle in the eye had remained, the remnant of what had been. In the evening, the doctors had given him his medication and the nurses readied his death bed.

Dunstan felt a feeling of coldness that began to rush up and down his arms and legs. The life-energy of his body contracted. Mack's heart went weaker and his circulation proceeded through a slowing process. He felt himself sinking into a pool of cold water, almost as if he had begun the process of dissolution. The soft hospital bed had perverted the departing energy flow.

Blackness swelled over him. Out of the blue, he actually believed he saw himself unconscious and surrounded by doctors and nurses. *That must be some other poor sap*, he thought. Dunstan cringed at the sight of tubes sticking out of the stranger's nose and mouth. *Poor bastard*, he mused some more. *Just say your prayers and eat your vitamins. You're a goner!*

Just like that, he realized that his speech came out slow, as if slurred, or drunken. As his spinal forces went upward, white, blue, and red energy emerged from the heart, pushing this spirit into the afterworld. He felt his arms and blood being burned by the life streams of fire. He felt his body descending into an area equal to that of a boiling point of water. He even felt the sensation of being pierced by an infinite number of hot needles. A great vibration now ensued. The life force departed between the eyebrows and many more of the parts of the body. As this energy gathered above his heart, he saw a great light shining above his heart.

While the forces traveled through the nerves, it took almost a half an hour to an hour for a multitude of such forces to reach the crown of the head, where a great heat of energy had risen and left the body. If only the doctor had not put so many drugs in his system. Dunstan now found himself overwhelmed by the hallucinations for as yet an unknown period of time. In such a conscious state, the dying man could hear the sound of his own beating heart. Unexpectedly, his heart beat no more, but he continued to breathe. He even heard voices whispering, but he knew not what they spoke, nor knew who they attempted to communicate to. He saw his wife Lydia crying, but a force prevented him from approaching her and giving her solace.

He felt himself rise from the darkness. His being almost froze before the intruding, dark clouds. He didn't want to die. He felt he still had it in him to fight these beings and the forces of nature combined. *I wish I could hold Lydia; just hold her one more time.* Everything seemed to slow down. Dunstan saw his whole life flash before him. He thought he saw a cave open up. Torches lined its walls and went on for infinity. Dunstan turned and jumped, shaken that he saw his own body stretched out on a bed nearby. Again he saw the parade of images that traveled through his mind, the early years when his mother and father had been together.

He even remembered the time when his mother remarried. He saw his stepfather Chet, a man who inspired him so many times, forever leaving a lasting impression on him. *Dad!*

Dunstan saw himself as a soldier in World War II. He also visualized a younger version of himself auditioning for plays and movies. He remembered speaking to Hal Wallis, who went on to help him become famous. All such events passed by him, until he descended to the underworld. For seven days, his ghost was lost in a dream-like state.

Dunstan was incapable of holding onto the clear white light of the beyond that would lead to the everlasting peace and non-being. When all his mental facilities had stopped, the mind ceased to create the divisions of illusionary separation. Thus, all became one.

He saw the whitest of all lights, the clear light of the beyond, and viewed the sun as a living being.

His kundalini was activated and it came in the guise of a shaft of light, which shot through the spinal column. Dunstan perceived it as his life force. He breathed lightly and his energies moved silently. Other forces then blasted through his body. The kundalini reached the highest part of the skull, which then radiated a glow. He systematically held his breath and drew his breath deeply, while inhaling with great force.

He held his breath; some energy did burst into flames, devouring his higher self. This process got him on to the path of the super consciousness, where he met a myriad of psychic guides. *Hey, how are you?* He would think, jokingly.

He discerned a great flash of light that penetrated all matter and energy. He saw the nameless god, in a formless and uncreated state. All the forces of his body now traveled through the many organs and glands, preparing for departure at the crown of the head. Unseen and unknown beings tried to guide the forces out of the body and through the crown of his head. Such forces traveled throughout all the chakras. Atoms and molecules were divided, sending out a sonic boom through the skull, leaving his eyes to flicker open. All the physical life forms of doctors, nurses, and loved ones disappeared into the background.

More mist obscured him and his surroundings. Dunstan then clenched his teeth. When one embarked on the land of the dead, one must be at peace with oneself and others.

In time, he penetrated the light of the universe, where billions of galaxies were born and died. Its brilliance was unknown, unborn, undying, uncreated, and consisting of raw mental energy, where fire and spirit had manifested. He saw the forces guide a mass of departing spirits into the next world, where men, women, and children of all ages passed through this golden light, becoming one.

Back in California, his adult children divided Dunstan's will. The best mortician in the business embalmed his body. Several hours after his death, they dressed his corpse in the best clothes that money could buy. In the evening, the media proclaimed the death of a screen legend. The next day, in all the newspapers and trade publications of that era, his obituary was proclaimed. In three days, unbeknown to Mack, he had a private funeral.

The ceremony consisted of a who's who affair, where politicians, former politicians, and celebrities were present. Tom Selleck delivered his eulogy.

In the weeks that followed, television networks celebrated Dunstan's life by playing all his old movies. Before his funeral, the obituaries appeared, lauded his legendary career, and then went into the annals of history. A&E even featured Dunstan's Biography. After the ceremony, the family had a private burial. Only close friends and business associates were invited. Initially, his family wished to bury the actor in his hometown of Michigan, but they settled with having his body interred at Westwood Memorial Park in the Corridor of Memories, alongside all the other Hollywood legends.

However, as Dunstan drifted further into the lands of the dead, the world moved on, and the actor descended deeper, where he became overwhelmed with hallucinations. Following his death, he could not detach himself from his riches, his desires, fears, and ambitions. *Where is my house and favorite chair? I knew I should have paid the Internal Revenue Service!* In time, he soon would learn that death acted like a mirror. If a man cannot let go of his possessions, his self, and his vices, hallucinations in the afterworld turned evil. As darkness encircled him, these hallucinations tortured him, causing him to yell and scream. When in a terrible moments of pain, his world went dark. Meanwhile, at such an interval, Mack saw a play, where his image was the principle actor. The dead man saw his life from a myriad of directions. He began to detest his egotism, his vanity, and greed. He watched himself break the destiny of his life that he had already lived. He projected himself back in time; also to those he had relationships. He saw the four courses of possibilities, which interested and eventually horrified him. Dunstan was lost in superimposing his world of dreams over his reality, which eventually bedeviled him in a world of illusion.

Dunstan soon became aware that he now possessed a body of energy; his earthly body was no more. At that time of realization, he encountered an ocean of light. He fought to maintain such a force. He tried vainly to handle onto this level of super consciousness. This newly departed tried to hang onto this pure energy, which came to be the source and return of all souls. As he passed through this ocean of light, where at some distance he saw a giant lake. A great edifice manifested, which shielded the unknown treasures of the underworld.

Each successive lake he passed represented a sojourn into the chakras. A lake of diamonds blinded him. He tried to cross this lake. If he did, he would experience bliss and non-being. He went further and saw a collection of suns, all varying in size and color. Each sun had a path into the white light, which came to be the state of oneness in the universe. They all represented a chakra. He must travel through its highest center and every path to escape this illusion. Dunstan struggled and couldn't let go of his guilt and sense of misgiving.

Unwittingly, he had failed at crossing each path and went into a higher level of consciousness. Dunstan now faced a grayish lake. As he stood on those dismal shores, he looked toward the horizon, where all his fears, desires, all feelings of guilt and desperation manifested, the site of his lesser self. Those who wanted to become, or have been. All his desires were realized, which would eventually become a source of agony after judgment.

A blinding light shocked our hero. A myriad of beings manifested, all statuesque, grand, and sublime. Their images chiseled from marble and physical features possessed an awe inspiring glow. Thus Dunstan had failed to overcome the self, inducing such great beings to arise from the oblivion— the judges of heaven and hell. Many native tribes believed people don't die, they transform into other animals. This would explain the shape shifting beings that populated the underworld. These entities took on the images of a set of

Supreme Court justices. The specters shaped shifted into the shape of alligators, or extraterrestrials. "We sentence you to be among the damned!" it cried. "You will never leave this world unless you have redeemed yourself."

Oh great! "Who are you!" Dunstan countered. "What did I do!"

His reaction and further pleadings of innocence was ignored.

"We have spoken," they pronounced. "All will be, will be as if you have not been at all," they proclaimed in unison. When a thunderclap sounded up above, the tribunal disappeared. *What was that all about?*

CHAPTER TWO

This abrupt and unexplained sentence essentially came to be an obstacle, preventing his liberation. Essentially, this lake and its inhabitants appeared to be a world of illusion.

Dunstan felt he was dreaming. He saw his surroundings blurred. A familiar room manifested and he stood in a fog. *Where am I now?* His eyes attempted to scan his location, but he could see nothing in every direction. The fog dissipated and a figure materialized from the oblivion. It was tall and dressed in white from head to toe. The owlish face bespoke the sense of kindness and wisdom that this entity would impart. It possessed a cherry red face. Its grey hair trailed down to his waste. A gentle wind pushed his white robe, as a sale would flap in the wind. A warm energy came from this being, almost a regenerative and warm feeling too.

Dunstan realized he felt no pain, radiating a warm face, where he beamed a smile. He looked around, but his vision was still blurred. Although he was in a dreamlike state, Dunstan still felt pain. He tried to ignore the blurring of the vision. As time went on, the shock of death and the numbness that followed induced Dunstan to accept the fact that his mind and sense could not be one hundred percent. He felt a flash go off, obvious a nice vision. Several forms stood before him. The specters, all gray and with no features, were all dressed in the color black. Some, however, shaped shifted into a pack of wolves with ferocious faces and long fangs.

The American's face went tight. *An explanation has to be in order.* "What's going on?" His voice again sounded slurred, or drunken. The blurred, grey outline motioned a gesture. "This is a dream! This has to be a dream!" he hesitated. *This doesn't happen to me. This is not the usual!*

"If this is a dream," it replied. "Then just wake up."

Dunstan closed his eyes and clenched his teeth. His eyes blurred again.

The human forms scattered about him. Some were in suspended animation, while others went about their business. When the mist disappeared, his vision again went hazy.

"Perhaps I have lost my sanity?" he told the nothingness. "I am going absolutely mad! Do you people like that!" he beckoned to the oblivion.

He felt gripped by a great sense of consternation. Mack looked around searching for anyone, or anything that could release him from this terrible fate.

This has to be a dream! Dunstan gazed around at the swirling fog. Every bone and muscle in his body ached. A particle beam of light shone before him. "Do you seek help?" it asked. "I will guide you if need be."

The fog diminished and Dunstan stepped forward. On the edge, his breath became forced, as he shook. The old actor tried to grasp the hands of the ghost, but his hands went right through it. *These doctors and their medication.* A mist gathered around him and he groaned. Things went blurring again. He wanted to speak to Lydia, but she faded into the oblivion, whence she had come. He looked at the corpselike form, which had shuffled its feet. *What's going on here*? Dunstan blinked sporadically.

Suddenly, icy fingers grabbed him, causing him to recoil. He cried out and staggered with it. He saw she had been crying. Her eyes had become swollen lines etched across her old face, as her hair went white. Lydia's grief had not been kind to her.

"Take your stinking paws off me, you dirty ape!"
Dunstan as Col. George Taylor in the Planet of the Apes (1968)

Near him a grave and tomb stone manifested. He saw his name and dates etched on it. A wave of apprehension swept over him. *Oh my God!* "This can't be true!" He looked at the sea of flowers that decorated the scene.

Mack threw his hands akimbo and stared unblinkingly at the scene, not believing the reality dispensed to him. The form descended down into the grave, covered by blackness. Meanwhile, he entered the casket and stared at the corpse. Its cold face frozen in a tight mask like state. *Who knew how long it had been there, or maybe it had become part of the grand illusion of the other side.* Suddenly he slipped out of the coffin, screaming. *This is complete utter madness!* A great fog enveloped him, did not let go, and carried him to the surface, where it freed him. The spirit saw green foliage, making him feel like a kid from Michigan Woods again. Every breath he took, made him feel at ease and alive again. In time, his grave clothes were no more. He had a short sleeved shirt, white slacks, and sandals.

Another image manifested before the doomed soul. It gripped his shoulder reassuringly and subsequently removed his arm from Dunstan's shoulder and patted the actor's back. Lips unopened, he starred at the same owl faced stranger before him. The entity now wore a black robe. A gold sash was wrapped around his waist. He also wore sandals and a tunic to protect himself from the cold. Dunstan would learn that this envoy was sent to assist Dunstan to separate this world of illusion and guide him to the great, white light of the afterworld.

"Who are you?" the actor asked.

"I am nobody," it replied.

Born on October 15, 70 BC close to the city of Mantua in Italy, he went to school, where he proved he had a deep intellect. In his life, he studied law in Rome, Italy. After working as a lawyer in Roman courtrooms, he grew bored, and moved to Naples, Italy to study philosophy and literature. Somewhere along the road, he became a writer. In that era, Virgil had carved a niche in the literary world.

His final piece of literature took him eleven years to complete. As a matter of fact, he finished his last manuscript during a three-year trip that he had planned. On such a difficult trek to Greece and Asia, Virgil became seriously ill. Sometime afterwards, the famed poet died.

"Where are we going?"

"Wherever you go, you will always remain." *What's he talking about?*

"So what is next?"

"Follow me." *Where!*

"Very well." *He offered and what is there else to do!*

In the night sky, the underworld of Hades shone. As the mist wore on, a gray vapor settled on the surface. Thousand kilometer winds patrolled this horrid world. It possessed a Moon-like terrain, which was dominated by large impact craters. It also had large volcanoes, which were recently active. The apparent freshness of the large volcanoes suggested their formation came within the last billion years.

Hades' atmosphere was composed mostly of carbon dioxide, and surface temperatures that reached forty-five Celsius on the equator in mid-summer, but surprisingly got much colder. At these pressures and temperatures, water could not exist in liquid form on the surface.

In ancient times, liquid water was more prevalent on the Hades' surface. Its atmosphere was thicker and warmer in former times, and perhaps much like the Earth's early environment before the appearance of oxygen. In mythology and in scripture, many great figures have recorded a visit to such a place. The physical barrier, however, made it impossible for the common man to make it to the underworld, preventing explorers from traveling to lands of the dead.

Virgil and Dunstan descended. The two traveled through the heavens and hells, where chimeras came alive. If Dunstan had been free of negativity, he would let go of this terrible, unimaginative reality. Virgil led all the lost souls to realization. In time, the famed man released a multitude of energy beams and entities from his centers, leaving his body as being composed of raw, mental energy. The men passed a myriad of greedy gods, demons, and the shadows of the suffering. Virgil narrowed his eyes at the hallucinations and kept fast to bring his companion to a proper liberation.

In this journey, Virgil encouraged Dunstan not to punish himself and cross the lakes of chimeras to achieve a higher spiritual plane, where Dunstan's' liberation would be assured.

Unexpectedly, Virgil led the famous man into the atrium that opened up into Hell itself. Older and grander than the Roman Coliseum, the pyramids combined. This structure possessed an architecture designed by a mode of technology not yet known by man. Meanwhile, Mack immediately discerned the writing above the opening, where he got the perception of sounds of the earsplitting screams of the condemned souls. The damned burned in a sea of fire, but some came to be victims, beleaguered and harassed by the various insects and wasps that populated these horrid regions.

The men drew closer to the River Acheron, where a serpentine water formation stretched as far as the eye could see, into an old, wooded area, where grotesque rock formations abounded. Sulphur Dioxide burned in the air and the bodiless would routinely scream, or shriek out, hoping to alert the living on the doom that lay ahead.

Out of the blue, an area boatman manifested. Its captain stared at the now dead movie star and laughed a maniacal laugh. "You are a real piece of shit!" he cried. "Aren't you!" he nodded profusely, laughing some more. *Looks like quite a character*, Mack mused, as he nodded back. The captain's hands trembled as he put a cigarette to his cracked, white lips.

A great wind flashed the horrid region, throwing Dunstan to the ground. That instant, he hit the ground head first, letting a sharp flash hit him between the eyes. Blood gushed from him, as he sat on the area terrain. In a skip of a heartbeat, Dunstan regained his footing, composure, and looked to Virgil and the boat captain.

"Are you ok?" the guide asked, frowning. *Oh yes.*

"You should have checked the weather network! You fucker!" the captain raved. "Hopefully the next she blows, it will take you away, and we will be rid of you! Just like others before you, asshole!" *Such a colorful character!*

Without much ado, Dunstan looked at the Captain who stared back at the boatman, who just shook his head. "Is that true?" he quizzed the poet, who nodded, furtively.

What's that all about? The old mariner motioned for them to get in and Dunstan and the guide did so. As the boat moved from the shore, the sounds of shrieks, cries, and lamentations only increased. The sky here never shone and the cries never ceased. A great wind pushed the ocean swells high, as the boat rocked violently. When the harbor came to be out of sight, the sad boat was caught in a squall and a sudden fog. *Where are we? Where are we going!* This did not matter because the Captain grew up as a fisherman and he knew the water well.

"Welcome to the city of Hades," Virgil remarked.

"Why are they sounding so distressed? Where are they?"

Virgil turned to him and replied, sublimely, "In this state, we pass those who lived a life of mediocrity."

"I don't understand." *Sounds mysterious?*

"Their lives were so dull; they now are imprisoned by the vice of envy." *Very bizarre, yet this does resonate as truth.*

Bitter and anxious. Dark haired and white oval shaped faces with stunning, sculpted eyebrows. Dark hair, white, and big-eyed women. All these dark figures of men, women, and children, forever victims of rabid dogs, possessed felines, and overgrown rats. Such a sight caused Dunstan to sigh.

A figure emerged from the lingering mist. This short man had dark hair with brown eyes. The naked man was a Harvard Law Professor, who had done the same job his father and father's father had done. Only now in this terrible place, he faced hunger, the stings of insects, and the whims of nature.

"Hey!" he called to the boat that passed his barren island. "I can promise you the way to the Promised Land," he cried to the wayward travelers. The professor, however, now dirty, disheveled, and wild eyed. This son of privilege had no papers to mark, nor lectures to make, or students to teach. His life of idleness and luxury truly asserted his doom in the lands of the dead. Many shared his misery. They spent an eternity cursing themselves, their mothers and fathers, who brought them into the world.

As the boat passed this appalling locale, more damned individuals begged for mercy. In time, Virgil expressed indifference; Dunstan grimaced at this never ending, ghastly spectacle.

"You'll see many strange things." *I'll bet!*

"Ha!" the captain spat. "You'll soon join them! You filthy asshole!" he added. *Already have!*

As the journey progressed, the wind roared and obscured the voices of the damned. A great sleep touched Dunstan, taking his mind a million miles away.

CHAPTER THREE

Fork lightening filled the darkness, awakening Dunstan out of his brief slumber. He thought the cries of lost souls would end, but he had no promise of such solace, as he began to descend the terrible valley.

Rocks, cliffs, ledges, crevices, clefts, and cliffs—all passed by, as if in a blur. He lost his grip, slipped, stumbled, and fell. Dunstan fixed his look in Virgil's grim face, into the eyes which no longer appeared cold as stone, but overcome with pain. They turned to look at each other, and for an instance the importance of their mission returned. Both stood motionless, as once more Virgil's eyes went up in the distance. *This never ends.*

"Some have been here since the beginning of time, or even descendants of ancient Mars, or pre-historic Venus," Virgil muttered, absentmindedly.

They continued their sojourn along the woods. As a kid and adult, Dunstan never feared the forest lands. He remembered walking for hours in it. At one time, he actually asked a pilot in a private jet to take a detour, where he then flew over his hometown area, the Michigan woods.

As they progressed deeper into the forest, a great fire erupted in the distance, causing more cries. Several shades approached them. One wore a tunic, the other rags and indifferent to the strange and surreal landscape. That instant,

Dunstan recognized and greeted one of them, a legendary figure of Hollywood's golden age.

More specters confronted them, some mirroring a lion, deer, or even a Kangaroo. The form of Leo Gorcey stood out. In this terrible place, however, the Bowery Boys just stared at Dunstan. No one said a word. The entities walked together in the direction of a glistening illumination. Mist lingered about them and they arrived at the periphery of an old fortress. Great walls surrounded this structure, which was strategically placed overlooking a precipice. Here a river emptied into a spring, which fed a series of low land rivers.

In ancient times, native tribal leaders would send virgins in a canoe off the falls, appeasing the gods of the valley of the underworld.

The spirits journeyed further onto a road composed of ancient, volcanic rocks and arrived at a pasture, leading to the night hour.

This was underworld's best kept secret—a landscape rich in folklore and tradition, myth, mystery and legend, where abandoned cities and towns straight out of the pages of a history remained forgotten, and a reminder of a past age. It possessed the mediaeval art and culture of three civilizations—Roman, Hungarian and Saxon. While ancient citadels, fortified churches and castles stood guard over this gloomy, rugged wilderness, the outline of ice capped mountains were seen in the distance.

That evening, Dunstan took notice of men and women who plied their trade in the silent film era. The image of Buster Keaton manifested into sight. To Dunstan, Keaton seemed more of a grandfatherly figure, friendly and warm.

Dunstan looked further and discerned the legendary comedy team of Stan & Oliver, all dressed in white from top to bottom. They smiled at him.

As the two continued, Edgar Bergen, Jack Benny, Fanny Brice; and Bud Abbott and Lou Costello also took forms on this trek. No one said a word to each other. These great spirits were frozen in time.

They trudged up steep mounds of graves and eventually crossed a moraine and made it through a maze of tumbled rocks on the far side. The clouds rolled above and souls moaned down below. Dunstan maintained his pursuit of Virgil down the upper limits of the Second Circle of Hell. At this time, Dunstan remembered his motto from western films—*keep on, keeping on.*

A disheveled and chained barbarian advanced forward, spat out, and cursed several oaths at the approaching Phantoms. Its face was contorted with rage. Its body covered in soot and its clothes in rags and its conscience heavy. In October 2001, the authorities made him the first Homeland Security Advisor. The President established the Office of Homeland Security and the Homeland Security Council, following the tragic events of September 11.

The former Governor was raised in a working class family in veterans' public housing in Erie and earned a scholarship to Harvard, graduating with honors in 1967. After being drafted into the army, the former spirit served as an infantry staff sergeant in Vietnam, earning the Bronze Star for Valor. After returning to Pennsylvania, he earned his law degree and eventually came to be the first Vietnam combat veteran to be elected to Congress.

That all did not matter now, the blackened and hideous phantom had no more laws to proclaim, a mere shadow in the lands of the dead. Dunstan almost didn't recognize him. This man once wore two thousand-dollar suits, but that had since shriveled to rags. Some said that the body of Tom Ridge came never to be found when the Al Qaeda

Network detonated a nuclear arsenal in Washington DC in the second decade of the 21st century. In that terrible hour, the President, his advisors, the members of Congress, the senate, and all the citizens of that great city joined the land of the dead.

Virgil majestically raised his hand and motioned the now crazed man to be silent. "Give us peace," he uttered. "Let us pass." Ridges knees gave way, making him fall down on his buttocks, onto a neighboring wall, which was near collapse.

"Wow!

"What's wrong!"

"Who was that?"

"It doesn't matter."

The men passed by the specter and continued on their way.

"Take nothing seriously," he muttered, turning to Dunstan. "Especially me."

Virgil concealed his countenance from the terrible winds.

"Is this the way we all end up?"

"This is where the world is going."

In time, as they continued along the road, the two descended into a sea of darkness. A gray vapor even obscured the road ahead, nothing as far as the eye could see. That terrible wind from Hades froze every bone in his body. He remembered the life he led as an actor, where he chilled in the Spanish Guadarrama in the winter and the Sahara in the summer.

Exposed skin turned black. He also heard the winds torture the poor spirits. At times, he heard a dog howl, or a child scream. Hearing a child cry in this terrible region was always hard to bear. Sometimes he would turn back and search for the youngster. Other times, he would dismiss it as an illusion only added to his sufferings.

More time passed by. They partook of awe inspiring scenery that was fossil rich and formerly glacial covered. Now it had become an arid, lifeless riverbed. In time, with its past life in clear view once again, new desert life emerged. One could see lines of discolored trees in a crack-like pattern, similar to what one will see when an iceberg collapses. Now, lacking soil and water, the vegetation became malnourished. A process required rock-eating life and erosion to result in soil and water retention. In the past, some earthquakes created such desolate life in its wake. The evidence of change maybe immediate and visible, or came in time.

Somewhere along the way, the men discerned an old logging roads in a reforested area. They observed other forms rising. Suddenly, a myriad of shadows manifested, overwhelming Dunstan with the sight of wounded individuals. *This has to be a nightmare. This can't be happening!* Grown men called for their mothers, pregnant mothers prayed incessantly, as their children, all called out for help. A folksy face with a pipe stared back at him. That instant, their sorrows and misfortune induced Dunstan to black out.

An hour must have passed. He didn't know how long, but soon Virgil aroused him, who now showcased smelling sauce in his age-worn hands.

"Where am I?"

"We saw the land of the Gluttons, but . . ." He paused to scratch himself and smile a wistful smile.

"But what!" Dunstan begged, battling another dose of erratic winds. "But what!" he repeated, almost coughing.

"They had no room because so many were shot," his guide replied.

"Shot?" *Hasn't he heard of the Second Amendment!*

"The doctors let them die."

"Why!"

"They had no health insurance," Virgil replied, sighing, obviously confounded by the ignorance of the man who divided the Red Sea for movie audiences.

Virgil helped Dunstan up and watched him from a distance, as the actor stretched and gathered his senses. In time, as they proceeded down a path, which had footprints from many ages, they came to a great gate, built of iron.

"Welcome to the First Circle of Hell!" Virgil exclaimed.

More hours passed. Thunder beat in the sky and echoed in the valley below, an eerie fog settled on the men. These mists were pushed by the ever-present winds, a great dog-like beast wolfed aloud, revealing the presents of Cerberus. Its menacing nature induced Dunstan to freeze. *What is that?* This vicious beast guarded the entrance to Hades and kept the living from entering the world of the dead. According to Apollodorus, Cerberus had three heads of wild dogs, a dragon or serpent for a tail, and heads of snakes all over his back. Hesiod, though, said that Cerberus had fifty heads and devoured raw flesh.

Its blackened face sickened all. Its skin stank of corpses. The tongues stretched out, revealing the awfully blackened, yellow teeth. Its screams warned all. Those many horrid eyes that stared from the specter. Sulphur Dioxide always obscured it. Sometimes it welded lightening, or thunder. Thus, it oozed the stench of death, promised fear and paranoia to the dead, and a great sea of blood covered the ground it guarded.

That instant, the men faced the three dogs that waited. Their howls eclipsed the cries and moans of the lost souls. When the ghastly creature discerned their presents, it revealed its fangs.

CHAPTER FOUR

The men walked on the skulls of their ancestors and heard more voices begging for help. That instant, one skull suddenly came alive, making the two jump.

"I only asked for 25% interest per month and year," it screamed, which continually frightened the travelers. "I was a straight up front business man. They wanted to borrow money and I gave them the BEST DEAL in town."

"Capitalism at its best!" the men uttered in unison.

Finally comedy relief. "A loan shark in hell!" Dunstan quipped. "Who would have ever thought!"

They clambered a promontory and hastily rushed across a weather-beaten path, turning across a corner, where they saw several persons outstretched on the ground.

"There's one," Virgil said, pointing at the athletic figure. The kids all wore baggy pants and stylish clothing. Some even wore those nice, Nike shoes.

"It appears that they are wounded. Talk to one of them," Virgil encouraged. Dunstan crouched down at the muscular, young man. This fresh faced 17 year old loved sports, both basketball and football, and forever yearned to return to play in the big leagues.

This looks interesting! "Hey," he muttered. "How are you?"

"I know you."

Must be a recent arrival! "Who do you think I am?"

"You're the head of the NRA." *Bingo, you got me.*

Dunstan stared at the huge, bloodstains on the teen's shirt. "What's your name and where are you from?" he asked, suddenly.

Good eye. "My name is Damien and I am from Harlem."

"How did you come to be here?"

"Old folks in my area once said that members of the CIA used to sell drugs to the kids in my neighborhood."

I somehow know where this is going. "Don't say," Dunstan replied, frowning at the strange entity before him. *Keep talking.* "I had a scholarship to play in the NBA."

"What happened?"

"Where I grew up there were drug dealers, or Johns, murdered every day. What was some black kid in comparison to a rich man being brought to a hospital?

In his lifetime, Dunstan prided himself on participating on his involvement in the Civil Rights Era when he listened to Dr. Martin Luther King say the 'I have a Dream' speech, which he had said many times. Many times he could still visualize the March and speech from Lincoln Memorial.

He and a group of prominent actors actually attended the legendary event, getting as much media attention, which promoted the vision, the message of peace, and opportunity.

It saddened him still to be labeled a racist in the 90's when his protest led to Ice T getting his record contract terminated. Mack hated being called a racist, or a redneck. He attributed these insults to the prominence and existence of the Woman's Movement and to Political Correctness being promoted in places of higher learning, which he often lamented.

Here it comes. "I don't know, you tell me," Dunstan responded, going crimson.

"When you cut open your skin we all bleed red blood. Cut further and you will find all the same organs."

No argument there. "That's true," the actor replied, grunting.

"It all changes when you open your wallet, have nothing, and all the doctors look back with all their white faces."

Can't help you there—can I? Dunstan looked around and grimaced.

"That's why I believe every American has the right to bear arms," the actor replied, majestically.

"Twelve year olds shooting twelve year olds. Because that what happens in my area!" the teenager replied, indignantly, which this time made Dunstan go pale.

Whatever one can say, their opinions will NEVER change! "All I can say is I hope all those white faces at the State Department and the Rockefeller Center paid you well. Because you are going to see plenty of guys like me as you go along."

This can't be happening. Dunstan frowned, got up, and nodded to Damien.

"You keep well," he muttered, stepping behind Virgil, where he hid. "You keep well," he repeated, nervously.

"Shit!" the young man cursed. "A rich, white man like you would never listen to a poor nigger like me!" the teenager added. That instant, the red-faced man, who graced some of Hollywood's biggest films, stood in silence over his guilt.

"There are many more like him," Virgil whispered. *I'll talk to them ALL if I can.*

"I know. I am sure," Dunstan replied, resembling a shamefaced man.

"I am used to running into rabid fans. I've dealt with people like that before," Dunstan added, still struggling with the embarrassment of being confronted. In his lifetime, the celebrity never had an entourage and dealt with people one at a time. In the big scheme of things, this encounter could be perceived as insignificant, yet Dunstan felt stung. He possessed a sense of shame since this meeting. He didn't know if he would interpret it as guilt, or compliance, for that youth's suffering, but if he did, he brushed it all under the carpet. He secretly dreaded what lay ahead. The sun went behind a mountain, leaving a shadow. In time, after a search, they found a level place and a shelter for a camp site where they pitched some tents. When they finished eating, it grew colder. *Who would ever think—hades of all places!* Virgil smoked his pipe and the two stared out into the darkness, where they saw the blurred outline of forests and valleys. Their bones froze under the surge of Artic type winds. In time, they dropped to sleep. The last thing he heard before falling asleep proved to be Virgil breathing, close beside him, under a separate set of blankets. At dawn, they rose, making use of the daylight. In minutes, both men laced their boots, dissembled the tents, rolled up the blankets, and plodded onwards.

LETTER TO THE NY TIMES
Printed May 12, 1998

. . . The Founders' intent in framing the Second Amendment is perfectly clear and undeniable. Thomas Jefferson wrote, "No man shall ever be debarred the use of arms." Some anti-gun elitists declare this notion outdated. However, many constitutional scholars from this country's most prestigious universities agree that the Founders' intent is clear and irreversible: To "keep and bear arms" is a right for all law-abiding citizens . . .

The next day, they trekked through the path chiseled, by a long dried up riverbed. The ghosts passed more shadows imprisoned by their pride, envy, and avarice. They crisscrossed a serpentine passage through a ridge, which contained a layer of metal-bearing rock. The phantoms continued to go down from a higher place towards a winding path. A ruined castle marked the border of one old dynasty and their arrival at the Second Circle of Hell. The men each gave a sudden, involuntary jerk and moved suddenly, making their way along the melancholic avenue where wind currents came crashing down on them and the terrible disfigured citizens who populated this region.

The sound of gunfire filled the air. A great gathering of restless spirits manifested, all originating from rings of fire.

"What's going on?" *Here it comes!*

"It's the way it's always been."

"Why don't you people organize?" *Why not now!*

"Organize into what?" *Groups!*

He discerned how many struggled against each other. Some were chained by the rockslides. They saw others pushed and whipped by unseen forces. Some attacked their fellow spirits with no provocation.

"Hope you have good health insurance!" one screamed to another, while drawing a gun.

"Right to bear arms!" another demon replied.

This has to be one terrible dream! Dunstan kept his face covered and looked furtively to the strange scene.

"What is going on here?" *Shall I hazard to ask?*

"Your actions in the previous world have thrown this world upside down," Virgil argued.

Alright! "When did this happen?"

"It's the way it's always been."

The men fled this locale and traversed through a series of boiling springs, which flooded into a long narrow trench dug into the earth. They pursued a long a bumpy, zig zaggy descent. Along a muddy stream, they saw cannibals from the amazon dining on another hapless victim. *Oh couldn't they eat out of a grocery store!* The smell of the cooking flesh almost induced Dunstan to vomit. They continued on this trek where they caught sight of a myriad of bogs which had long since trapped souls in its grasps. Shadows in the polluted waters preyed on wayward travelers. The rivers thickened into blood.

In the distance the travelers discerned a flash in the skies above them. A man made beacon flashed a holographic image in the sky. These images came in the guise of hieroglyphics. Another image responded to the signal tower. Both modern and ancient mariners used this form of communication to eliminate collisions in the myriad of waterways.

The morning gave way into the afternoon. They followed the channel and the men stopped by a strange figure emerging from the rivers of blood. This person was unimposing, anxious, and high strung. The form had a broken nose and its forearms were covered in tattooed flames. In its life on earth, the specter once was white, in his 20's with a brown goatee and a large gap between his teeth. They exchanged greetings and salutations.

"Who are you?" they asked.

"Nobody," it replied.

"I just got my driver's license and drove across the country."

"Are you American?

"No, sir, I am Canadian," it answered, but continued in a matter of fact way, by saying: "I got to Vancouver. No sooner did I cross the border, and then I was car-jacked."

Could see this coming from a mile away! "When was this?' Dunstan asked.

"July 25, 1995," it replied. "They all had assault rifles and surrounded the car. When they found out I had no American money, they shot me."

This is where experience is a MUST! "Now if you were allowed quick and easy access to guns, would you still be here," Dunstan ventured.

"What the fuck do I need a gun for!" it screamed. "All I know this is not my time to go!" it added, holding its head in despair. *The only good anti-gun advocate is a dead one!* No sooner than the ghastly shape appeared, then it went forever under the surface, whence it had come.

"In its lifetime, this man was destined to be a bank manager, like his father," Virgil mused, smiling at the irony. "It's full of fury that its life was stolen away in a moment, "he added, without shaking his look of irony, which was etched all over his face. "He was just trying to do something different in life." *Right to bear arms!* In the background, they saw the contour of a fortress, where a metropolis existed, one of the most bustling destinations of the underworld. In ancient times this mountain Spa, situated above sea level, at one time was the center for business and commerce. It also possessed a labyrinth of caves and catacombs, which could be explored over a few weeks. The location also possessed rare and a variety of flora. Native tribes used to hunt and fish, or conduct outdoor religious rituals. Old, wooden churches and monasteries now remained hidden in the scenery, possessing art treasures of unknown wealth and quantity.

An educated observer would note the great architectural value of the numerous castles and buildings. A fortress from antiquity even housed a busy, thriving community. This nation state preserved an old and authentic folk art. Its inhabitants wore red and black embroideries. Dunstan observed their sleeveless sheepskin coats which were made by their furriers.

These citizens possessed a war-like demeanor. All around them, great, faceless barbarians whipped slaves, whom passed by in a variety of directions. This experience evoked memories of the films he played in. He actually remembered his days on '*The Ten Commandments.*' In his mind, he could not escape the memory of peasants staring at him pass on the set, as he played Moses. Thousands of peasants eyed him, as he walked along the streets, wearing only a tunic and holding a staff. He shook this memory when he saw a familiar face, his friend and legendary actor, Vincent Price—the King of Horror Movies. *I know him!*

For the meantime, Price continued to look down from a charcoal stained edifice, yelling, "Mack! Mack!" *What!*

Anybody who knew Dunstan knew that he never liked to be called by his stage name. His wife didn't even call him Mack. Everyone called him Max. It made him nervous to hear someone calling him otherwise.

"Mack!"

This can't be him! "What!"

In an instant, Price gestured to a long, narrow opening in the rock, which led to a threshold into the old civilization. A midget saluted the screen legend, before delivering an obscene gesture. "Welcome, Mr. Dunstan, you filthy bastard!" *Diplomacy and this man do not mix!*

In life, the men had been friends for over fifty years. As a matter of fact, Dunstan had said many times, he had no friends, he just knew people he worked with for decades.

A group of hulking figures came forward, entreating Dunstan to travel alone in Hades. The old actor shook his head at all such offers and preferred the companionship and direction of his much sought after guide. Out of the blue, the encroaching figures forced the great barrier shut. Virgil stood pensive, trying to form a response in his mind. He took several strides back and forward, and then stopped abruptly.

Virgil stood motionless and speechless. His body and mind seemed frozen, as his mind seemed a bit off. This guide seemed oblivious of any movement behind him. Such ideas appeared new to him and his indecisiveness showed on his face. For perhaps half an hour, he moved. On such walks, he moved slow, mechanical steps.

"I demand to be admitted!" Virgil asked aloud. "I demand to know why I am prevented access!" he added, creasing his brow with frustration. Virgil sighed and Dunstan stared at the hieroglyphics that decorated the stone. He then climbed down a set of granite stairways, which led him descending a slope, where an urban type environment began. This milieu appeared filled with mountaineers, all around with packs, muskets, and possessing travel bags.

Unexpectedly, at once, a forty-five year old pizza deliverer came forward. This personage had a razor thin figure with bushy sideburns.

"Hey!" he quizzed.

"Can I help you, sir?" *This looks fun!*

"I was taking my girl out on a date. We drove to a Drive In. Somebody got it into their head to hold up the place."

Here it comes. "What happened?" Dunstan ventured.

Please continue, sir. "I tried to stop them. A fourteen-year-old shot me point blank range. I will never be there for my little girl."

"Did they find the killers?"

"He stole the gun from an uncle who was a long time member of the NRA," it replied, pointing a long finger at Dunstan. *I certainly asked for it.* "I'm glad you're here," it whispered, but still it continued. "To get what you deserve. I think you're such a crook. And I hope you never leave here!" No sooner than it expressed its point of view; it disappeared into the hustle and bustle of this strange town.

Right to bear arms! Virgil came forward and Dunstan nodded.

Very well. "Has anyone ever gone this far?"

"This is the way it's always been." *This man will never answer a direct question.*

Just like that, Medusa came forward. Medusa, originally the Serpent-Goddess of the Libyan Amazons, possessed dread locks, long leg, and garish attire clothed her body. She resembled an out of work exotic dancer. A goalie mask concealed her face. No one could look upon her face without glimpsing one's own death as she saw your future.

"Don't look at me," she warned.

Live one here. "Why?" he replied.

"She will turn you to stone," Virgil interrupted. "Take her warnings seriously." *Sounds like my woman.*

"You will never return," the entity added. "You will never return," she repeated, with a heavy Moroccan accent. *I certainly meet them all.*

Another night came and went. Thunder shuddered above. A terrible wind pushed through the woods and an explosion of flames appeared inexplicably, causing the habitants of this underworld to shake. Men the size of tree trunks at one time populated this region. They moved with agility and speed. They continued down the narrow, cobblestoned streets. Dunstan discerned more shadows that emerged from the road. They proceeded past a great edifice, which was known as one of the strongest fortresses in the underworld. Its White and Black Tower hearkened back to the Gothic Era. This church once possessed the grandest organ and the most famous organist. In the remote past, its hallowed halls had been retrofitted with the most riches of carpets, complete with an imposing building with an interior tower built afterwards. Spots of ivy now obscured the soot that had remained on the walls from the big fire, since lost from memory.

He caught sight of an old cemetery, where the travelers observed the bodies of the dead lying in open graves. As a matter of fact, he even recognized these faces as members of the anti-gun lobby.

This is a strange one. "Why are there graves in hell?"

"You'll learn more as you go along," Virgil replied. *A real politician.*

Out of the blackness, a body rose from a grave. *This will never end.* "I recognized your voice, sir," someone ejaculated. "Who are you again?" it chirped.

To add to his horror, Virgil jumped beside Dunstan, mumbling: "Please watch what you say to the souls in this area they can be quite violent," he urged. *He only warns about this now?*

Dunstan looked to the man with the fat, honest face, and walrus mustache. *Looks like a nice man.*

"Please tell me about yourself?"

"I was a butcher in Queens New York. Put my kids through school. One night I took the night's earnings to the bank."

Is this for real! "Were you robbed?" *This has to be a nightmare.*

"The bank was robbed; I was shot, and rushed to hospital." *This can't be happening!*

Right to bear arms! "What happened then?"

"The doctors refused to treat me because I had insufficient, health coverage."

"Sorry to hear that, sir."

"I hope the money was worth it."

"What money?"

"The weapon's industry paid you," it screeched. "It was blood money!" it added, sneering derisively at him. *Who gives these people such ideas?*

"I don't know what you are talking about!" Dunstan replied, indignantly.

"You went from 'Planet of the Apes' to the leader of the NRA," it accused, full of anger, and disdain. "You did not deserve such a movie career!" it raged. *I worked hard for it.*

Dunstan went on to argue how every American has the rights to bear arms. He also supported his point of view by quoting the constitution. The form would have nothing more to do with this debate, ending the argument on one final affront—flatulence, before disappearing.

Well I give him once ounce of credit, he mused. *He had the last word.*

MSNBC TV

September 14, 1997

. . . The First Amendment is crucial. Of course it is. So are all the others. And the Second Amendment is the one that guarantees that people can bear arms to protect themselves . . .

CHAPTER FIVE

A council square sat behind a hill, derelict and forgotten. This structure beheld an old tower, positioned strategically where it watched over who entered its territories. The foundation and the ground floor of the tower remained. Once it used to be the center of the Town hall. To the ground floor of the tower, one could find the History Museum where art exhibits once hung. Only shadows occupied it now and called it home.

The next day, the stench of burning flesh filled their nostrils. The two had long since gained access to the Third Circle of Hell. They approached a bend in the road, which made them rise over a series of hills, where they climbed down an incline.

In this territory, burnt out tanks and cars littered the roadside. Here, they came to the long since forgotten grave of William Randolph Hearst, the grandfather of tabloid journalism. The spirits followed the direction of the incline into the Third Circles of Hell through the formations of a long defunct volcano. In a skip of a beat, they heard a roar that emanated from a very deep crack in the earth, a seemingly endless or measureless chasm. *Must now awaken the dead!* These travelers ran past the break, they took refuge in a stone structure, once the remnants of a ruined castle situated on the high rocky hill. This thousand year old structure helped to provide defense against the then Turkish enemies.

This stronghold once belonged to a great, powerful King. His successor rebuilt and enlarged the upper castle and added the lower castle. Large parts of its walls had remained until this present moment. The North walls remained preserved. The lower castle then rebuilt still provided its renaissance elements, such as sculptured windows. Unfortunately, in the twentieth century it had the misfortune of being invaded by the Russian and German military machines. It has since fallen into disrepair. The last inhabitants left many years ago and have not returned since.

Dunstan pointed at the serpentine river which bubbled sulfur from the deep.

"What is that?" he jumped. *This looks interesting.*

"We are in the lands of the volcano." *Sounds different too.*

Armed men drove in an army jeep. These entities once guerilla rebels that had fought in a long forgotten Honduras War.

"Hands up!" one of the men screamed. *O great!* "Or we'll shoot you where you stand!" *Who will question the right to bear arms now?*

Virgil held his hands up and nodded. "We are unarmed," he retorted. *With good reason!*

They demanded where the famed escort held his allegiance, but Virgil remained silent, as he stood motionless and speechless. His very body and mind appeared mechanical, almost equal to a toy soldier under a Christmas tree. When the jeep drove off, Virgil pointed at the spirits in the background. "Charles Manson, Jeffery Damier, and Ted Bundy occupy this level," Virgil mused. "Jack the Ripper too." *A virtual whose who. Where is my tux when I need it!*

"Really?"

"Yes, and there are many like them too."

A mist came down on the bleak landscape. Nearby the Tyrants of history remained, all imprisoned in a burning river, where the flames reached their eyeballs.

The fog still lingered, as the men followed a weather beaten path into a wilderness where trees dwarfed the adventurers. The size of the trees never induced Dunstan to fear. He loved trees and even enjoyed the sounds and smells of chopping wood. The travelers continued, however, to see many things. They heard unimaginable sounding mating calls between grotesque humanoids, which resembled half-human and half animals. Long extinct dinosaurs populated this place too. As they continued, the foliage got denser.

"Be careful what you touch and where you go," Virgil warned him. *It is obviously that this isn't Disney Land.*

"Oh!" Dunstan replied. "I think I can handle myself."

That instant, he moved his hands along a natural decoration of leaves and branches. Suddenly, he broke just a small twig and a female voice shrieked; almost making his heart beat so fast and jump out of its containing walls. *What the devil is this?*

"What the hell was that!" he jumped.

"We are in the lands of the suicides," Virgil replied, mechanically. *This place doesn't come with a travelogue.*

The mere twig he had just snapped now bled crimson, human blood. In time, the strange conversation with the offended entity made this situation more surreal. It went as follows:

"Why did you do that to me!" it shrieked again.

"Who are you!" the actor replied, his face etched with shock. *The most overly connected, Hollywood hack couldn't come up with script like this.*

"I am the tree you imbecile!"

"Trees don't speak."

"Well I do!" she rejoined.

Well the ones I knew took the vow of silence. "Who are you?" he inquired, frowning. *Almost like a children's show!*

In minutes, the tree explained her history, where she was the daughter of Greek Immigrants, who settled in the Bronx. In a fleeting moment, he imagined the image of a short, pudgy girl with pretty blue eyes. In high school, her friends called her '*Goodie,*' indicative of her ability to avoid all forms of wickedness. She constantly referred to herself as Rosetta. She always fantasized about working for the foreign affairs department and being stationed in an exotic locale. Eventually, Rosetta studied political science at Columbia University. She then got involved with a government program, where she worked as an intern for a U.S congressman in Washington D.C. When she graduated from school, she got hired as an executive assistant. This job became her life—away from her family, her friends, and became not only the confident of her distinguished employer, but his mistress too.

When *Goodie* got pregnant, he forced her to have an abortion. Six months later, he dumped her, and the girl was fired. She could not face going back home with this terrible shame. The person who found her dead was the maid. Since her old boss had roots in the CIA, her body was dumped in a field outside of the city, which had a reputation for being the dumping ground for murdered prostitutes. The maid also went missing, but that didn't matter because nobody gave her disappearance much thought, or concern.

In time, the National Enquirer hired a private investigator, which then went on to discover a love letter, forcing the congressman to resign. As the weeks passed by, an investigation was launched, attempting to satisfy the concerns of Rosette's grieving family. Presently, however, the tormented spirit found herself condemned to live out her remaining years of her life in the lands of the suicides. After this story was told, Virgil then looked at the bleeding branch. "The truth will set you free," he said, quietly. *Why did he say that for*?

"No!" she moaned. "Forget about me! I am lost!" she begged. "Just leave me alone! Leave me alone!"

As they heard the sounds of her crying, the great tree bled further.

"Just look into the light." *Maybe something will come of this.*

"No!" she screamed.

"Just look into the light," he implored, gently. *Maybe this chance encounter means something in the big picture.*

The tree shook with such violence. Lightening shone above, causing clouds to move, revealing a falling star, or meteorite. "The truth will set you free," he murmured again, almost whispering.

In the blink of an eye, a dark figure lurched in the woods. Two popping sounds followed. It then disappeared. In its place a tiny tree amongst the forest. "They come all the time. At all hours. Every day of the year," Virgil muttered. *All from the worlds above.*

As the night went on, the two proceeded further; Dunstan again had the misfortune of meeting another tortured soul. This time its entombment resembled a lowly bush.

"Who goes there!" it quizzed aloud. *Another one*!

"We are merely passing through," Virgil responded, diplomatically. "We are sorry for intruding."

Dunstan shrugged and suppressed a mild laugh. "So tell us about you," he ventured. *This could be a good one.*

The spirit in the plant began to elaborate on how it lost its investments on Wall Street, all due to corporate corruption and wrong doing. His grief was compounded when he learned his wife had cancer of the uterus. For years she had tried to have children and had suffered several miscarriages. This required many rounds of chemotherapy and medical treatment. He had no health insurance. Since he could not qualify for a bank loan and they owned so little land, he went to a moneylender. He got into debt. This finally led them to the brink of mortality. They owned only a car. He took a hose, inserted it in his car tail pipe, rolled it open, and affixed the other end through the passenger window. They had fallen behind in rent many months previous and faced an eviction notice. He honestly felt nobody would notice him gone from his job at the warehouse.

Meanwhile, at that exact moment, Virgil looked intently at the rose bush and said, emphatically: "The truth will set you free." *All giving peace to the restless and forgotten.*

"No it won't!" it harangued. *He will.*

"Why don't you just look into the light?" he again entreated. "The truth will set you free." *If only life were that simple back home—we would achieve world peace, instead of war and famine.*

The bush moved violently, as if afflicted by the presence of a person. It burned and disappeared into the ground. The only remnant of this strange spectacle came to be the charcoal stained soil, which added to their melancholy. "The truth will set you free," they muttered in unison. *It certainly has.*

After some rest, they dissembled the tents, ate, and departed this haunted land and moved across the desert landscape, where no animals, trees, plants, or spirits dwelt. The desert had a history of healing. Moses, Jesus, Mommed, Buddha, and others all felt its power, as he did now. That morning, a great wind blew in their faces. No one spoke for a long time. Lost in thought, exposure to this environment helped Dunstan to look back on his life. He thought of the people he knew, the life he led, and his regrets. He cherished the memories of drawing sketches with the family at the site of an ancient ruin, in Europe, or elsewhere. Dunstan enjoyed being a Father. He loved driving his daughter to ballet and watching his wife teach the kids how to swim. And he had adventurous children. They explored the pyramids in Egypt and Mexico. They saw wild animals in Middle America and overseas. They explored old ruins, heard music in Vienna, and saw Shakespeare in Stratford. His son Fraser met his future wife, Maryle Pernfuss on the Princess line cruises. His son eventually married the stunning blonde on a bluff overlooking Vancouver Sound. His daughter Holly went on to marry Carlton Rochel, a rising star at Sotheby's. His daughters' wedding came to be celebrated at St. Thomas Episcopal Church on Fifth Avenue, where the proud father read out the Song of Solomon.

"Marriage is the ultimate compromise," Mack once said, before he celebrated his 50th wedding anniversary. "It really is," he added. This celebration took place at Dikko Hotel. All family members on both sides of the family were present, including his half-sister Kay. They made Jolly West master of ceremonies. Mel Torme sang "Our love is here to stay." Friends, politicians, enemies, actors, Generals, senators, and Tom Selleck all came to the celebration. He even remembered his mother passing away at age ninety-six, her cremation and her ashes being scattered on a bridge near the Maple Street hove, over a quiet canal flowing into Lake Michigan. *Yes Max had a good life.*

Several minutes later, they saw a motley colored group that manifested from the blowing sand. *Now what do we have here*! In minutes, one of its members descended on them and quickly recognized the movie star. This specter had long, dark hair, and green luminous eyes. It nodded and shook the celebrities' hand.

"I'm your number one fan." *Really*?

"Who are you?" he asked, unduly horrified at the fact of being recognized. Although he lived his life in the public eye, Dunstan relished his time alone. He actually hated parties with large amounts of peoples. Whenever he encountered such a situation, he would wander to a bookshelf. He would rather read the titles on the spines of those books, than be centralized at such a gathering.

CHAPTER SIX

In the past, Virgil routinely warned Max about meeting other travelers in the underworld. He often spoke of how some succumbed to terrible acts of violence.

"How did you come to be here?" *This man has a story to be told. Let's let him say his peace.*

"I entered a great ship and eventually found myself here," the form responded. "I wish I watched all your movies, but I died too soon." *This sounds strange.*

Virgil frowned at this admission and constantly spoke of how Hades came to be replete with liars, thieves, and cannibals, who would lead you off your destined path to devour you.

"I will remember the tremendous talent you brought to the film and the television medium." *Never miss the flattery!*

"I just consider myself a working actor, nothing else."

"Really!" *That's about it.*

The men exchanged good words, pleasantries, and parted ways. The spirits now moved down a depressed slope, which Virgil announced as the Fourth Circle of Hell. *Not even a stewardess, or customs official!* There they saw a dozen gullies, as hard as rock, where no animals or plants dwelled. Virgil spoke of the history of the region. Each bridge like structure they passed was made of a thin, bamboo and rope.

In the afternoon, the image of a great fortress manifested. It possessed a series of trenches, where the bridge hung over. Sometime along the way, Dunstan passed the first bridge; he saw several faces that he recognized. As a matter of fact, Dunstan observed a man wearing greasy pants and having long hair pulled back into a ponytail under a New York Yankees cap.

I know this person from somewhere, he muttered to himself. *I swear I do!*

As he narrowed his eyes, he saw further into the squalor, which beheld a crowd of naked blondes bathing in boiling Jacuzzis. *What have we here?*

"These are the pimps," Virgil ejaculated. If it is too good to be true . . .

All of a sudden, Max again stopped, staring intently at the facial features—none other than Larry Flynt. *I know him*! Gradually, Max observed another familiar face. Hugh Hefner strolled about, smoking a pipe and dressed in a bed robe.

Hef, the publisher of Playboy magazine, became known to have created the world-famous Playboy Mansion of Los Angeles in 1971.

Hefner strolled the grounds in his jammies, pipe and smoking jacket, nodding his approval. Some famous and unknown Playboy bunnies surrounded Hefner. Around him were a myriad of fans and false friends, which induced the guide to etch his face with such disgust and contempt for the preceding individuals.

The spirits exchanged greeting and pleasantries. Dunstan turned to frown on why the living intruded on his journey through Hades.

"Time distortion," Virgil surmised. *What! Where does he come up with these things*!

"What do you mean by that?"

"Why bother living if things, or such things, are pre-ordained?" Dunstan argued. "It is absurd!" he lamented.

In time, as they crossed another bridge, Virgil nudged Mr. Dunstan to look down below. In the farthest corner, the travelers observed a strange manifestation. They beheld the Robber Barons in their glory. Their beings now trembled, their voices quaked, as they illuminated from a nearby pool of methane which shone into the perpetual night sky.

The Captains of Industry! "Well!" Dunstan smiled. "I'm not the only Republican in hell! There are more here too!"

He looked to Virgil, who assented. "You're telling me hell is a 24 X 7 Republican Convention?" *With good credit too!*

"Basically." *Maybe God is truly a Liberal Democrat?*

As the afternoon wore on, they passed over another ridge, where they discerned some of the souls trapped in a pool of feces.

"Who are they?"

"Flatterers." *They have their place too?*

One voice stood out from the rest of them—the one and only Joan Rivers and her daughter Melissa. This mother and daughter team interviewed celebrities on the red carpet. In her life, three dogs accompanied her in public and on television, all dressed in expensive dog fashions with matching accessories. "Can we talk?!" she screamed. *I don't think so!* This sight induced Dunstan to laugh a voltarean laugh.

Had to let it out! Couldn't hold it any longer! "Joan Rivers is certainly getting the red carpet treatment," he uttered, smiling again. *And some!*

"Hey!" the Queen of Barbs screamed. "What are you looking at!" *Sorry not tonight.*

They quickly fled the plight of the River's clan and crossed another bridge. The men then passed through an old battle field where the dead moaned and doomed soldiers called out for their long dead mothers to help to calm their never ending pains. He saw many swollen faces and rudimentary stitches from foreheads to cheeks, bloodied faces, and arms, all holding bodies together. *How can we give the dead their comfort? There is so many.* Burnt out tanks and cars littered this thin, cobble stoned path. Dunstan shook his head at this terrible scene and remembered the days he enjoyed in the USO.

Wherever he traveled, he always made time for the troops. During the Vietnam War, he visited Vietnam, and met a group of wounded soldiers. At a moment's reflection he collected the telephone numbers of their loved ones. When he got home, he called every number. He must have spoken to over three hundred, girlfriends. A movie studio even supplied a phone and office to make the telephone calls.

When they passed this terrible scene, Virgil stopped abruptly. "Those hands and feet below." *We got something now?*

"What now."

"Those hands and feet below," he repeated, pointing downwards. Dunstan squinted his eyes and caught sight of a crowd burning in a river down below. Virgil continued to point his arms majestically at these poor wretches.

"They were people at one time." *Certainly.*

"Who were they?"

"Merchants in the temple."

Something to do with religion? "From scripture?"

"Go down and talk to them."

Here we go again. Dunstan sighed and followed a path that led to the bottom of the path in the sour, burning stream.

"Who are you?" a burning spirit asked.

Who am I again? "Nobody," Dunstan replied. "I am nobody. Who are you?" he countered. *Asking a question to a question sounds like a politician.*

This answer met him with indifference. Pat Robertson, a fixture of the Religious Right, stared right back at him. This blackened and burning man had once been involved in a scandal in which he used donations from Operation Blessing to fund his diamond mine in Zaire.

"The feminist agenda is not about equal rights for women," he once said. "It is about a socialist, anti-family political movement that encourages women to leave their husbands, kill their children, practice witchcraft, destroy capitalism, and become lesbians."

Jimmy Swaggert and Pat Robertson now burned side by side. Swaggart gave out emotional filled pleas for money *to carry on the Lord's work*. In the 90's, his meal ticket ended when he got caught in a motel room with prostitute Tammy Faye Baker.

Roberts, Swaggart, and many of their prominent members of the American Christian Right burned here. Their accountants, stockbrokers, and their whores all joined them in the lamentations. As a matter of fact, in the 80's, Tele-evangelists collected millions of dollars for starving children, then flew to Africa to be filmed kissing previously disinfected dying babies. Then they flew back to America, showed the footage on television and collected more millions. Contrary to the dogma that they promoted, they misappropriated between 85 and 95 cents of every dollar collected, much of which ended up in high-risk speculative commodity accounts in New York and Chicago.

At one time, the IRS demanded to see the financial records of these television preachers, but their sudden refusal, and subsequent fall out induced the authorities to cease their inquiry. *These men are sleazebags, a mystery in itself.* Dunstan somehow knew that he faced such personages. He also somehow knew that these men had no desire to be freed. He wondered why but left this for another time. In time, Virgil and Dunstan left the moneyed ministers to their forever suffering and torment.

That evening, the phantoms crossed the Fifth Bridge, where the two were overwhelmed with the sight of boiling water. On Virgil's advice, the travelers had them hide behind an old marble column from ancient times. Out of the blue, a dark figure emerged from the darkness, casting a small entity into the water, which caused screams. Without warning, Virgil went forward and confronted the faceless demon.

"Who are you!" he demanded. *Didn't he warn me about such direct contact?*

All of a sudden, it lunged at him with a pitchfork.

"Who are you!" he asked again.

The spirit stopped and breathed in and out, its lungs filling and emptying. This diminutive character stood five foot five in height. In life, the official resided in a palatial mansion in Washington behind a phalanx of security guards. On official visits a detachment of secret service agents were present. The once soft spoken man had lost his human form and took on that of a reptile. The afterlife had not been kind to him.

At the height of the Cold War, Paul Nitze was a central figure, who negotiated arms control with the then Soviet

Union. In all actuality, he virtually destroyed the armament and nuclear containment negotiations in Geneva in 1982. Nitze accomplished such a dastardly dead in place of a previous negotiator who had successful come close to signing an accord. Nitze only answered to his boss, the then Secretary of State George Shultz, a former chairman and majority shareholder of Bechtel Corporation, America's largest defense contractor. Therefore, Nitze directly influenced an arms race between America and the USSR in the 70's and 80's, when money and resources could have been set aside to fight poverty and famine in Africa.

"I did what I was supposed to do." *I bet you did!*

"What did you do?"

"I was only doing what Washington was telling me!" it protested. "I obeyed my orders!" *It had to be bad* for you to land up here!

"Do you seek forgiveness?" *Don't think so.*

"No!" it fired back, with almost a glint of vengeance in its response.

In the meantime, the demon pointed and warned the travelers that the six bridges were severely damaged and his gang would lead them safely without payment, or reward. *Let's hope so!* Later, that night, they resumed walking through a dark wood; a shadow suddenly ran through Dunstan, making him jump. *What the hell was that!* They passed by boiling streams, rivers, and lakes. All of which contained many condemned souls. *These poor people. Is there no end to their suffering!?*

Suddenly, the light disappeared and maniacal laughs could be heard. *There must be something coming up!* The creatures stared, their eyes replete with the flicker of flames and their blackened bodies were armed with machine guns. One of them, a mischievous midget, sported a pitchfork and a tight smile. Many times these entities shape shifted into leopards and cheetahs, all welding weapons that constantly awakened into snakes. *This is unimaginable, yet is happening.*

"This is the end of the road for you, Virgil," one of them admonished the guide. *Our ticket is up!* The devils looked at Dunstan and ruminated on attacking him. *We are done for!*

"Look into the light," Virgil whispered, but the creatures did not move.

"Never!" Nitz screamed. *That won't work!*

"Just look into the light," he whispered again.

"Never! Never!" it shrieked, repeatedly.

"It's where the world is going."

CHAPTER SEVEN

The ghoulish and ghastly characters went into a huddle, and argued amongst themselves. Their voices never sounded above a whisper. They uttered curses and threats, but Nitz stood, and faced our heroes and said, dejectedly:

"Ok you're in. We'll take you."

"What are your conditions?"

"We will take you to the Six Bridge unharmed."

That instant, the strange creatures all uttered a suppressed, fiendish laugh. The poet waved them to be silent. *In such a circumstance, the truth is an inconvenience.*

"When did the bridge collapse?" Virgil asked, astutely.

"When nuclear clouds appeared over Washington and Europe," they replied, laughing almost hysterically. The highwaymen continued another wave of indescribable laughter, Nitz then gestured them to be silent. The garishly attired and grotesque group scattered ahead, inducing the famous men to pick up their pace.

"Nuclear clouds over Washington," Dunstan mused aloud. "You don't suppose the world ended?"

"Impossible." *What!*

"Why you say that?"

"The world is a forever spirit," Virgil replied, solemnly and assertively. *This man has an answer for everything. American TV would love him!*

As their strange allies hurried up ahead, Dunstan reminisced about Hollywood. That split second, they saw stragglers who avoided a confrontation with the demons by jumping into a nearby boiling ditch. This gave their protectors a moment of rest, where they lost themselves in long maniacal laughter and guffaws. One devil remained hearing the duo, pursuing at a distance.

Around this time, one of the group members revealed his past. In WWII, Marquis Ito was employed as an envoy for the Japanese government. This senior Japanese Diplomat had extensive field experience and was respected by his peers. A year before the bombs were thrown onto Hiroshima and Nagasaki, the Japanese Government sent him to the West to surrender Japan. None of the allies would recognize his credentials, and even the International Red Cross Organization in Geneva failed to act in this matter. When the bombs exploded over Hiroshima and Nagasaki, Japan finally had an opportunity to surrender.

He recalled traveling to America, where he was assigned to offer Japan's unconditional surrender. They astounded him by refusing his historic gesture with indifference. Ito still blamed himself, ignoring any argument suggesting otherwise.

An image manifested in Dunstan's mind. It happened just for a second, but its effect resonated.

He saw airmen on their way to bomb the mainland of Japan. *Oh my God!* The warriors manipulated a few knobs on their control panels and watched the readings of the altimeter. Out of the belly came what looked like a black object and it fell downward.

On August 6, 1945, American warplanes dropped the first uranium atomic bomb, on Hiroshima killing over 140,000 people. On August 9, a plutonium atomic bomb was dropped on Nagasaki, killing over 75,000 people. Marguis Ito never forgave himself for it. The mist and grey vapor obscured such a scene from the past.

"Why don't you just stare into the white light?" *This won't help*!

"Never!"

He can't possibly blame himself. "It wasn't your fault!" Dunstan interrupted. *He won't listen to rhyme, or reason! This is crazy*!

"Impossible!" it cried.

The drop of the A-bomb on Hiroshima officially ended hostilities in Japan. He unequivocally refused forgiveness and chose an eternity in Hades, as opposed to being freed of his terrible guilt.

In WWII, a young Dunstan was drafted into the army. He decided to go into the air force, which enabled him to continue his studies. While training in the forces, he learned Morse code and aerial gunnery. In that period of his life, military officials told him that he would be going to fight in China, Burma, or India. In 1944, however, he and other soldiers packed inside a truck, which drove along a wet road. When they arrived at the harbor, they boarded a frigate which took them to the Aleutian Islands, which was barren and possessed an active volcano. He saw no action, but experienced tension caused only by the absence of women. Dunstan always thought the dropping of those two atom bombs saved his life and others too. After he spoke with Mr. Ito, he knew better.

The next day, they once again took down their tents and journeyed onwards.

All of a sudden, one shadow leapt from a chasm in the ground and threatened to attack. *What can this be?* As it materialized, it formed a Caucasian man with a shaved head. It met defiance from the gang, who then chased him into another dimension, where the image disappeared forever. Moments later, as they neared a ridge, Virgil excused himself. *Let the man have a private moment.* The Poet went ahead and slide down a slide, which led to the appearance of a set of solemn individuals, all indifferent to him. He then came to a burning lake and stared at it. Here he set his eyes at the formerly known Reverend, Billy Graham, a famous, twentieth century evangelists.

Graham now accompanied his son, their stockbrokers, their profit projections, and all their whores forever to cook, until their guilt burned all away.

Dunstan slide down to Virgil and the devils remained on top, laughing at the wretches in the river, where our heroes now stood. "Why don't these men want to be freed?"

At this time, Virgil explained that the leaders of the American Christian Right and the Evangelists, all collected billions of dollars from the faithful, and they gave a minimal amount of their money to feed the starving children of the world. "In the 80's, when a famine was raging in Africa, these men flew on Private Jets to the starving masses."

"What happened then?"

Virgil explained that in the 80's, 25 to 30 million children starved per year.

"Whenever an evangelist died, they were always met by the starving masses."

This is incredible! "How horrid!"

"Hell is an illusion."

This sounds crazy! "What do you mean by that?"

Virgil got animated whenever he revealed the mysteries and the very workings of the underworld.

"Whatever your vices, it will mirror it."

This doesn't make sense. "Please explain."

"If you are a drug baron, you will feel the sensations and the pains of every drug addict and that of their families, until you are cleansed of such bad karma."

"So Billy Graham, Pat Robertson, Rev. Jerry Falwell, and all the tele-evangelists will suffer the pains of every starving child?" *They got exactly what they deserved.*

"They landed in Africa on a private jet, had their whores sanitize the starving children before having them appear on American television."

"Wow!"

"When they collected the money from the sheep, the merchants in the temple climbed back onto their private jets and flew back to their palatial mansions."

"Less than ten percent of it went to feed the hungry?" Dunstan remarked. *This has to be all hearsay and conjecture. None of it can be proven. In fact, this in ITSELF can be an illusion.*

CHAPTER EIGHT

As a dinosaur bird dived bombed them, the traveler's made their way, seeking refuge in the rocky terrain. "If you see somebody from the business, please tell me," Dunstan chortled. *As if such a request would be granted.*

They then passed through a clearing. Two shades then came forward. One wore a skull bandana over his dreadlocks; the other had a rugged feature and slanted eyes. The spirits revealed themselves and imparted the fact that they were the fake priests of the PTL fame. The travelers now stared at the ghosts before them. In their eyes, they could see the scene of the crucifixion of unknown persons, which induced Dunstan to grimace. In his lifetime, Dunstan took his work seriously. In school, the director of the play casted him as a nephew of Christ. He always concerned this as an omen of predestation. After that performance, he was awarded a scholarship to Northwestern University. This all led to Dunstan being offered a role in a school film, *ambitious but doable.* And he never looked back.

As he continued to stare into the dead eyes, he remembered working on Ben-Hur and the weight of the crucifixion scene, which induced Max to tears. Claude Heater had played the dying savior in that scene. Heater never was seen on screen, but still his performance not only contributed to the movie, but moved his fellow actor to tears.

The things you remember! "How horrifying!" he replied, covering his eyes.

That moment, the phantoms parted ways.

"Never believe what you see, or hear."

This is puzzling to no end! "Why!"

"Nothing is for real."

Whatever he says will never make sense. "Why do you keep saying that!" Dunstan quizzed, recovering from the sense of shock.

"We are in the lands of liars and thieves," Virgil replied.

FOX News Channel May 18, 1997

... He [President Clinton] boasts about 186,000 people denied firearms under the Brady Law rules. The Brady Law has been in force for three years. In that time, they have prosecuted seven people and put three of them in prison. You know, the President has entertained more felons than that at fundraising coffees in the White House, for Pete's sake ...

That evening, they found a level place and shelter enough for a camp site, where they set up two tents. Dunstan watched Virgil with troubled eyes. He started to speak, changed his mind, and they went silent. Virgil had set up the oil stove, and sorted out the remaining food. Mack had stubble on his beard, looked pale, and sunken. Dunstan possessed brooding lips, dull eyes, and felt completely worn out. *This has to be a nightmare!* In time, he raised the flap and crept into the tent. In a heartbeat, he removed his boots, and rested down on his blanket. Dunstan lay in torment. *When will this ever end! Must be a nightmare! When will this all ever end!* As it grew colder, their bones frozen under the surge of constant artic type winds. The wind stalked the terrain; the darkness crept in, as Virgil breathed in and out nearby.

They now entered a great mist that obscured them. Freakish weather patterns tortured the landscape and its inhabitants. The heroes had a difficult time mounting the boulder of a fallen bridge. In time, they zig zagged slowly up the long incline. Almost every move must be planned. As time passed, the slope resembled a wall, where they climbed. They stood up, staring into the bottomless cavern. They set out a way to pass it. In a flash, they espied a bridge that spanned the crevice. They followed a path that ended in a climbable wall, forcing them to turn. Thus their progress became slow and steady. Both men continued to study the terrain, the slope, and the cliff that lay on either side of them. Dunstan head jerked up, where the brightness became darkness.

The legend barely made it up to the collapsed bridge. After they succeeded in making it through this obstacle, the guide motioned for a resting Dunstan to continue.

This is never ending. "Why?" the American asked, taking a deep breath. "Why can't we rest for just a minute?"

"Highwaymen abound."

Certainly no rest for the wicked. "You saying we have bigger fish to fry?" Dunstan replied, mounting from his hunches and walking forward.

As they climbed a mountain road, strange voices came from the chasm below. In it, they saw snakes and grotesque reptiles from the dinosaur era. One snake leapt from this horrid scene and tried to attack them.

Houston, we have a problem. "Watch out!" Dunstan yelled, almost jumping. No sooner the animal faced them; it then burned to ashes, screaming a strange language.

Here we go again. "You will see many strange things," Virgil muttered. "The worst is yet to come." *This man and his subtleties.*

That afternoon, when they left the great fog, the two came to the Lands of the Criticizers. Here they saw Gene Siskel and Roger Ebert manifest. Ebert was armed with a big bag of popcorn, with extra butter. These movie critics argued amongst themselves. They cursed themselves, their show, and the Hollywood system, where the movie franchises had eclipsed the art of cinema. In time, other critics appeared and disappeared. Some famous and other from obscure, third rate magazines. During this interval, the serpents and the reptiles then devoured these men. *Alright, I always thought those two were a bit odd.*

The duo mounted a long, narrow chain of hills, and came to an area where two slopes met. At this junction, they saw sulfur dioxide that rose from the various cracks in the surface. All along the mountain walls small flames, flickered in the wind, kept alive through an unknown or mysterious source. That instant, Virgil spun around and faced the American, who marveled at the scene. *Where are we?*

"Welcome to the lands of the deceivers," the guide muttered, almost laughing. *Oh, got to keep on your toes for this one!*

In a heartbeat, they passed through this land. In each flame contained a burning soul. In their eyes, one could see their tale of woe and regret. Dunstan saw media magnets, presidents for life, and the Prime Ministers, who they had bought. The CEO's of Enron and World com found a place, including their drug addicted sons and daughters too. Drug barons and Finance Ministers all knew each other well in this illusion. Their whores also joined them in the flames.

In the sky above, long dead armies marched in the sky. Soldiers crashed into soldiers, causing great bloodshed for far as the eyes could see. Sometimes, Dunstan stopped by happenstance and viewed an old colleague in the NRA who glowed in the flames. *Poor devil!* Out of the blue, he caught sight of Marlene Dietrich, before she vanished from view forever.

That evening, at the next bridge, Dunstan passed through a bombed out hospital, where patients were in stretchers in the emergency rooms. The medical staff had left the sick to die. At one time, the building had extremely tight security, enclosed by a gate, with bullet proof windows. All visitors buzzed in at reception. Today, however, all the wounded ranged from age eight to seventy-one. Some sustained wounds in their knees, groins, abdomens, and shoulders. Others suffered from incurable diseases. "These people need medical attention," Dunstan cried, looking at a wounded twelve-year-old boy, who sat beside his pregnant, fourteen-year-old sister. *Who, or what, rules this upside down world!* "Jesus Christ! Where are the doctors or nurses!" he yelled at an empty corridor, his voice echoing. A closed sign hung where a nursing station stood vacant.

"At the height of the Cold War, one trillion dollars was spent a year on hiring over half the world's scientists to make and design bombs," Virgil rattled off, sighing at the ghastly sight of a wounded, night watchman. "All the money that would of gone for America to maintain a free, universal healthcare system, instead went to stockpile weapons, which may, or have yet to be used, even when the Cold War was won," he added, grimacing at more misery. Afro-American, Hispanic, or those from the lower class, remained in this place of misfortune. Most of the wounded were children from the ghettoes, or from Government Housing Units.

What else can be said? "Is this the future?"

"It's where the world is going." *This rational again?*

This grisly multitude all had their stories to tell, but in time the men moved on, avoiding such cries for help.

Dunstan remembered his old life and his death experience that opened up this reality to him. All the hospitals of all the lands stared back at the mere god looking at his creation.

"Welcome to Mack Dunstan's Inferno!" Virgil cried, almost unable to control his great voltarean laugh. *Oh, blaming me for this—are we!* "If you go further enough, you'll find Saddam Hussein's weapons of mass destruction," Virgil continued. "All his weapons are made in America. You know that?" he quizzed Dunstan, almost enjoying regaling his famous fellow traveler with interesting anecdotes. *More conspiracy theories!* That split second, his unusually animated guide further spoke on the occasion when power brokers acted on President's behalf, inviting the future dictator to New York, where they wined and dined him. The monster even partook on viewing a Broadway play. This led to Hussein to commission artists to write plays, or books, all of which credited to him. *Such a story maybe false, or even true. Who is to say?*

The ever-present smell of sulfur dioxide helped the hours pass by slowly. Later that night, they came across a ground whose borders annexed the final circle of Hades, the location from scripture, where men, women, and all the poor souls fell from a height into a sea of fire, burning for an eternity. *Such a sight to behold, if not to run away from.*

"So what's up next?" *Never ending.*

"I know not what you speak." *More of that rational.*

"Where from here?" *There must be some point to this journey.*

"You will see many, strange things." *This is an understatement.*

In time, the fog thickened and held them in a grasp. Lightening filled the sky. Thunder drummed up above and the four winds of the universe continued to harass the inhabitants of this strange land. Darkness even overwhelmed the land. Great ice flows broke apart, condemning lost soldiers and sailors to perish forever. They saw an ancient, nuclear wasteland. *Would never think there was a snowballs chance in hell was possible*, Dunstan chortled, smiling at the bitter irony of it all.

"Welcome to the lost victims of Atlantis," Virgil announced. "Entombed forever in the remains of a comet that hit earth in the ancient past." *Even they have a story forever untold and unknown.*

In the meantime, they then caught sight of frozen figures in the ice and those who murdered family members. In this desert wasteland, he witnessed a strange manifestation.

A great gathering of beings congregated before a group of judges in a make shift courtroom. Apparently the whole terrain was littered with bombed out homes and buildings. The whole city was laid to waste by unseen forces. These phantoms came to replay the past, where they condemned the monsters of humanity.

Those who faced prosecution here were ordinary everyday individuals, good fathers, caring to animals, and even unassuming. In fact, each individual had committed unspeakable crimes.

This trial featured men who couldn't fully appreciate the human consequences of their career-motivated decisions. In time, a myriad of defendants attended these trials. During this hearing, the judges heard first hand witness accounts of horrific acts of war. Some escaped trial and punishment in their lifetime, but eventually these captured entities would be indicted. That moment, a bright specter stood sublimely before the gathering of forms. "What we propose is to punish acts which have been regarded as criminal since the time of Cain and have been so written in every civilized code," it spoketh, eloquently. Seconds later, the ghost delegates then disputed whether to proceed using a simple jury trial, or a set of judges.

As a myriad of images faded into the darkness, the shape of the proceedings came to be clearer. The hearing court then heralded itself as the Underworld Military Tribunal, and it included one primary and one alternate judge from each country.

CHAPTER NINE

Sulphur dioxide hung in the air. The stage had been set and the actors were in place. As the trial began, more forms filled the old city, or what remained of it in the lands of the dead. Carrion birds manifested, who then went on to represent members of the prosecution and defendants, where the now dead gathered. These ghouls then went through the whole process of interviewing potential witnesses. They also went on to identify imaginary documents. All lawyers, regardless of which side they represented, interviewed their clients and began trial preparation. More apparitions came, representing the members of the world press.

Dunstan and Virgil quietly watched the war criminals take their seats in the docket. At one time a sage-green draped and dark paneled room existed behind them, but only shadows remained in a barren wasteland. Positioned behind the figures stood six American sentries with their backs facing the beyond.

"Attention! All rise," A Peacock type character shouted. "The tribunal will now enter." In an instant, the judges from the four countries glided to their spots, where the benches once stood. A pulsating light rapped his gavel. "This trial, which is now to begin," the English lion stated, sublimely. "It is unique in the annals of jurisprudence." *This is an understatement.* The ceremony amongst the ghostly figures now took their places in Hades.

An invisible entity now read out the indictments. "Conspiracy to wage aggressive war," it said. "Waging an aggressive war against peace."

"War crimes and crimes against humanity," said another voice.

An orange being delivered its opening statement for the prosecution. "The wrongs which we seek to condemn and punish have been so calculated, so malignant, and so devastating that this civilization cannot tolerate such abuses being ignored because it could not survive there to be repeated," he spoke to the beings, who remained silent.

As the trial progressed, the prosecution continued to stimulate cries of outrage and gasps from the ghostly spectators. Evidence was brought forward, suggesting that the offending leaders of a country knowingly appointed a dictator, trained its military, and armed its militia. Such evidence portrayed the ruling government as corrupt and barbaric. *Do things ever change?*

Somehow the specters set up the technology to show Film footage, which gave a visual image of the barbaric crimes that purported to have been committed. This entire apparition lasted only a few minutes, but its appearance left an unsettling taste in the mouths of the observers.

When the Defense presented their case, more forms came to the stand. Some came to the stand unrepentant. Others evaded questions and gave no apologies.

"Once we came to power," he said. "We were determined to hold on to it under all circumstances," one of them said, showing no remorse. *Sounds like Hitler, Stalin, and Mussolini combined.*

More images and forms passed over the strange gathering. Rodents for each of the defendants presented their evidence. In most cases, the defendants themselves took the stand, trying to put their actions in a positive light as possible. Many of the defendants claimed to know nothing of the secret payments to higher officials. A man with a yellow stain in the middle of his Santa Clause beard returned a thoughtful gaze. Around him tattoos, beer bellies, and pony tails made him appear at home. Another tugged on a goatee.

"Are you saying that you did not know about the terrorist training camps?"

"I knew nothing about that."

Prosecutors then produced maps in an effort to prove that comment was as a blatant lie, or just inaccurate. In time, other defendants testified that they were following orders. A few of the defendants confessed their mistakes and offered apologies for their actions. *What a pity!*

An ex-American president now took the stand. *This is unheard of! This NEVER happens!* "Have you ever participated in the selling of weapons to the enemy?" *This has to be a nightmare.*

"My conscience does not allow me simply to throw the responsibility simply on minor people," it replied. "I did what I was told to do, nothing more nothing less." *Unbelievable this is! Can't be real by a long shot-definitely an illusion!*

The Defense Minister then came to the stand. "This war has brought an inconceivable catastrophe," it testified, "Therefore; it is my unquestionable duty to assume my share of responsibility for the disaster that came on the American people." *The world must have ended. No questions about it!*

Ghosts and shadows came and went with little fanfare. The gathering of spirits increased in size for the much-anticipated closing arguments.

A majestic, Bald Eagle stood before the gathering, concluding his summation with a passage from Shakespeare. Dunstan mouthed the words when spoken, wetting his appetite for Shakespeare under such strange conditions. This actor always felt the continually study of theatre was futile. He also felt it should be applied to the real world—live theatre, or the production business. When he moved to New York, he auditioned for Broadway plays and lived with his friend Bruce Marcus in Brooklyn. Later on while his wife worked as a model, he survived on a veteran bonus.

He actually worked $1.25 an hour as a model, posing for art students. In this job, he would run Shakespeare soliloquy in his head to alleviate the boredom. He constantly circulated his pictures and resumes across Broadway and Manhattan. He remembered going on one cattle call where he did a cold reading of a Shakespeare play. They did not cast him as the lead in Anthony and Cleopatra, but as a simple officer. He found acting in Shakespeare plays drained one of their energies. Dunstan actually acted with Godfrey Tearle, who went on acting even though he had suffered through a bout of the flue. When Tearle left the stage, he could be found vomiting into a bucket, yet maintaining a high caliber of performance in a known, difficult play. That all didn't matter now, as Dunstan and his fellow travelers watched a bizarre ritual, where spirits played out the events of their lives, much like actors did on a theatre stage.

More ghosts came and went. Soon after, strange images and sounds manifested over the presiding gathering. Some defendants offered apologies and wept but others offered a strong warning, alluding to the dawn of twenty-first century man. "This trial must contribute to the prevention of wars in the future," someone said. "May God bless the United States of America!" *No argument from me!*

In moments they would know the verdicts of the tribunal. A lawyer manifested and told the defendants that they must remain seated while he announced the verdicts. He began with an American President: "The defendant, the former leader of the United States, was the moving force for an aggressive war, second to no one . . . . He let the powerbrokers appoint leaders of the enemies, they helped train terrorists, and arm them."

As fog settled over the specters, lightening filled the sky. In a flash, more ghosts came and went. A great wind then blew the balls of light about. The court, its proceedings, and the many men and animals condemned to replay history all vanished into the pages of history.

It almost felt like time had forgotten this land and the people that lived here. The world passed it by, unconcerned by their pain and suffering. Several moments later, Virgil and Dunstan then traveled through the depths of hell to the center of the earth. On this journey, they saw many ghostly shapes of the departed.

The next day, Dunstan set up with a jerk, pulling his boots up without lacing them. He dropped the flap and turned away. His lips looked compressed into a thin, bloodless line and his hands opened and closed at his sides. Above them, the rocks rose bleakly into grey stillness. Mack cupped his hands and yodeled. *That felt good!* His fists clenched to whiteness and he throbbed in his temple. That moment, he felt an unmistakable change in his bones, blood, and his heart. They studied the rocks and chose their route and began to climb. After a brief rest, they moved on.

They soon came across the most famous of all traitors to humanity—Lucifer. According to Christen lore, before the creation of Adam, the civilizations of humanity existed on the terrestrial planets. Some have alluded to the belief that angels created habitations on the Earth, Mars, the planet Venus, and the Moon. Others have suggested that God did not create confusion, but order out of nothing. Satan on the other hand, corrupted what God had already created in perfection. When Satan rebelled, God casted him down as profane from the height of heaven. The rebellion of Satan plunged all creation into a state of corruption, where before it had been perfect and glorified. When Satan and his angels rebelled, God wrought destruction on the heads of the rebellious "sons", with power that cannot be imagined. After the devastation of Satan's kingdoms, many of the rebellious angels were bound and held until the time of judgment, or so we have been told.

Around them, the erratic weather patterns pounded the lands and its peoples that called it home. Virgil and Dunstan never exchanged a single word, but followed a buried road to the surface. In time, they entered a series of tunnels, some of which was small, leaving them to squeeze through. The famous banged their heads on the walls and ceilings, expressing their frustrations against the gods for undertaking such a long, at times, fruitless journey. Eventually, this maze opened up to a giant cavern. Somewhere in this bleak land a weak light shone up ahead, revealing the vestige of the Mount of Purgatory.

"Welcome to Lucifer's tomb."

Here? Really! I should have baked a cake! "Is he here, or buried here?" *Maybe we can get his autograph.*

"This passage was created when he fell from Paradise."

A photo finish. "Wow!" Dunstan replied. "We should say a prayer for him in remembrance," he added, jokingly.

On the N.R.A.'s. Trigger locks?

"A ludicrous invention. If you can't put it on a weapon without taking the bullets out, why put it on?" A five-day waiting period? "It's hard for me to accept that a guy says, 'I'm going to kill that SOB, but, darn, I have this five-day waiting period.' He probably still wants to kill him after five days." Ban Saturday-night specials? "The black and Hispanic women who clean office buildings until 3 a.m. and then walk home—of course, they want a handgun in their purse." Limit purchases to one gun a month? "It's the camel's nose in the tent. Look at Stalin, Mussolini, Hitler, Mao Zedong, Pol Pot, Idi Amin—every one of these monsters, on seizing power, their first act was to confiscate all firearms in private hands . . ."

They went along a body of water that shape shifted into a channel. All day long, they pursued this course of this brook out of Hades to the land. It descended into a lower angle, where they stopped to face a mountain. In days since forgotten, the wise men christened this place 'Purgatory.'

In the spheres above, he saw an alien, star formation. They then left the horrors to enter their new kingdom. Seconds later, a dark, cloaked inhuman figure emerged from the island. *What do we have here?* "Who are you who have left the lands of the underworld," it asked aloud, its voice screeching.

At least it's friendly. "Who are you?" Virgil, replied, tactfully.

Out of the blue, the stranger evaporated into a sea of molecules and atoms. Several feet away from where they stood a bush began to burn, leaving Virgil's face to go rigid.

The guide then walked a stiffened walk to a set of reeds. Dunstan followed behind, his face etched with concern.

Must be sorcery. "What are you doing?" Dunstan muttered. "What do we do now?"

"Alas, our journey will not end now, but continue," Virgil replied. *Such is our fate.*

CHAPTER TEN

They rested, burning some wood by the riverside. At dawn, a group of pilgrimages approached the traveler.

"Where is the path in the mountainside?" one of them ventured.

"We don't know," Mack replied, causing the men in the crowd to stop in fascination.

"Aren't you famous?" another asked.

The crowd gathered around Dunstan, satisfying his actor's ego. That instant, Max recognized someone—*Buddy Holly! This can't be so.*

This musician sported horn-rimmed black glasses. He died when his chartered plane crashed. His death came to be forever immortalized as 'The Day the Music Died' in the song 'American Pie' by Don McLean.

For the time being, someone in the gathering pointed to the heavens above, revealing a streak of light. In a flash, a spacecraft landed, a group of humanoids disembarked from the vessel and approached the pilgrims. *We got more friends.* In a heartbeat, the men from another society scrutinized every member of the group and stopped at Virgil, who saluted them.

"What do they want?" Dunstan quizzed him.

"They seek the way to speak to the dead." *Is this unusual!?*

The humanoids from the stars looked human enough. These beings, all bald and wearing metallic colored space suits came across as very conscious of contamination, and avoided close contact with every member of the dead, or supposed dead.

Let's welcome these space cadets. "Where are they from?"

"Ancient Venus," Virgil revealed. "It blew a part fourteen thousand years ago and laid planet Earth to waste," he added, melancholically.

Unbelievable. "Sorry guys!" Dunstan joked. "Come back in a million years." No one returned a smile at this suggestion.

Someone came forward, who was tall, lanky, and sporting a warm smile. He worked on an oilrig in Kuwait and died in an explosion in Gulf War I. Dennis came from a long line of military men. He loved military history and the whole life that came with it.

"I loved all your movies," he said. "Especially Planet of the Apes," it added, as it shifted into a cow like creature with wolf type face.

"Well thank you."

"On the other hand, my wife was not much of a fan of your stance on the NRA."

As this conversation began, Buddy Holly played with his guitar, strumming to the sound of everyone's clapping. In a flash, lightening streaked across the sky. It even started to rain. The small gathering walked along a well-worn path.

That moment, Dunstan noticed that Virgil had no shadow. This greatly perplexed and alarmed the American. "What's the matter?" Virgil murmured.

How can it be said? "Nothing."

"Don't you trust me anymore?"

The ship has not sailed yet. "It is not that!" Dunstan replied with exasperation. "You have no shadow!"

"That's the will of the gods," Virgil replied. "And they never remember. They are forever forgetful." *He has an answer for everything. Does Mr. Gloomy ever change?*

Unexpectedly, a great wind blew, pushing the clouds open, letting in a ray of sunshine that shone down on them. In another flash, a crowd moved toward the strange manifestation. The celestial particles beams induced the men to shrink. A shabby looking individual stopped to face Dunstan.

"Do you recognize me?"

Dunstan thought long and hard.

"Colin Powell," he guessed.

"That's right."

"They never listened to me."

Again more rabble. "Who?"

"All those people died because they didn't listen to me. I really tried. I really tried," he lamented, holding his head.

"What happened?' Dunstan begged. *Did the world end?*

"The nuclear annihilation of Washington," Virgil replied. "It's horrific aftermath."

"It was unimaginable, but it did happen," the general assented. "Fifty thousand dead in one blast too." *A good time to die.*

Very slowly, Dunstan approached Virgil and tried to find the right words. How can I say this without sounding to presumptuous?

"Did the world end?" *Must have.*

"Impossible."

How can he deny that? "Why do you say that?"

"The world is a forever spirit," Virgil replied. *If he's not gloomy, he's weird about it!*

As the men smoked, ate supper, and slept under their tents. Lightening emblazoned itself across the rolling clouds above. Sulfur dioxide continually rose from the surface.

The ridge broadened, buckled, and slanted skywards, resembling a vast ruined staircase. They pushed their bodies to the mountain, pushing their clothing and fingers to the flesh. As far as the eye could see, they discerned only rock and ice. As the hours passed by, the shadow still hovered about him. Fear soon gripped Dunstan. Fear far worse than falling; fear he had no experience before. A wave of emotions filled him, different from any before. He gripped the rock with his arms, legs, and body weight. Minutes felt like hours. His eyes shut and trousers became torn. His fingers bled. His eyes looked before him, as the slope moved upwards. Eventually, a deep fierce joy swelled in his heart. The coldness had returned into his bones and blood. Moment by moment this shadow and human overwhelmed him. He felt his body battered and his clothing torn. Blinding snow streamed like needles into his eyes. A hail of rocks came down upon him. Thundered sounded. Dunstan found a hollowed out section of rock with it, side and top projected upwards. The small cave offered a place of refuge from the infirmities. That night, the rocks were slippery with rain.

The climb required much effort. In order to make it through, the men used both hands, as they held onto some parts of the mountain. In time, somehow they made it through the path. As they traveled, they even heard a distant murmuring and the groan of the mountain. Dunstan stopped to breath, perplexed not only by the position of the sun, but the makeup of the constellation that shone in the night sky.

"The universe affects the outcome of world events."

"What caused it?"

"In ancient times, the earth was hit by a comet, or asteroid," Virgil spoke.

"That would also affect the dead?"

"Basically." *How?*

The two stopped abruptly. The two each agreed an unexplainable force, or energy barred their passage forward.

"It's not a magnetic field?"

"No."

"Then what is it then?" *So very strange.*

"In order to pass, one must free themselves of hate, anger, and guilt."

Dunstan argued that he possessed no such feelings, and their impasse resulted from unknown, supernatural phenomena.

"The penitent man will pass," Virgil insisted, almost making the now departed laugh.

"Sorry for what?" he quipped. *Must be an angry spirit.*

"We all have anger, hate, or guilt buried in our heart," Virgil argued. "It's what makes us as individuals. It's who we are. You're no different."

NBC "Meet the Press"
May 18, 1997

. . . Let me make a short, opening, blanket comment. There are no good guns. There are no bad guns. Any gun in the hands of a bad man is a bad thing. Any gun in the hands of a decent person is no threat to anybody—except bad people . . .

. . . Teddy Roosevelt hunted in the last century with a semiautomatic rifle. Most deer rifles are semiautomatic . . . it's become a demonized phrase. The media distorts that and the public ill understands it . . .

. . . You know, the Bill of Rights guarantees every citizen the right to own and bear firearms. It doesn't say anything about how many, how much you can pay for them. That's in the Bill of Rights. That's a sacred document in our country. There's no other country in the world that has such document. And you know what its purpose is? To prevent the federal government from interfering with private citizens' rights . . . If you will read what the Founding Fathers wrote when they were writing it— Jefferson, Mason, Madison, Patrick Henry, Tom Paine—every one of them wrote at great length that they were talking about the individual rights of individual citizens . . .

. . . We have to pass on to America in the 21st century the same Bill of Rights that those wise, old, dead white guys that invented this country passed on to us . . .

Dunstan continually argued that he possessed no such negative attributes. Since the guide was so insistent, they agreed to stop for supper and meditation. Half an hour later, after their meal, the men position themselves in the yogic position, where they conducted breathing exercises. The view they partook heightened their state of meditation. Meanwhile, as they continued through this roadside ritual, the mountain seemed to go higher, breathing through the clouds. In time, they saw the ledge had disappeared and immediately reached the mountaintop.

"Where are we?" *I felt a shift in my being. I know I did!*

"The obstruction is gone." *Must be magic.*

In the meantime, Virgil examined the geography and locations of the sun in relation to the moon and stars. That instant, Dunstan jumped to notice that the mountains and monuments came in line with the stars in the sky.

How am I supposed to say it! "I suppose it will get easier as we go along?" *Fingers are crossed in this one!*

"I know not what you speak." *Again with the double talk.*

As meteors broke up through the sky, the men continued to journey upwards towards the constellations in the night sky. In the morning, a group of cowboys came forward. They cleared their tent, had their breakfast, and departed. The apparitions were traveling in a caravan. When Cecil Demille casted Dunstan into "The Greatest Show on Earth," Demille wanted to actually take the cast and crew on the road to capture what goes on in a Ringling Brothers, Barnum, and Baileys circus. Old movies were usually filmed on studio lots, but Demille preferred location shooting to get exterior shots. He even had the actors learn the circus stunts and perform them, thus making the movie authentic. They moved in a caravan to get that motion picture done. That production traveled across the country in cages, wagons, and trains, the way circuses usually traveled. Demille succeeded, capturing the entire experience on film and it will never be done like that again. *For the record books!*

In a skip of a beat, Dunstan noticed Virgil had a shadow again and this made him cheer. *The positions of the planets have been kind to us once again.* This outburst attracted members of this caravan over to them. "How'd, partner!" one called out, slapping his pal on the side of the back. These persons all radiated smiles and toothless grins. *Friendly country folks too.*

"How are you!" another retorted, bowing.

As time went on, some of the group members became convinced that they recognized the celebrity. Hollywood legend has it Demille was in Rome staring at a portrait of Moses and his assistant pointed out the physical resemblance that Dunstan shared with Moses. Many have said Dunstan bore a resemblance to a lot of men that he played. Maybe great men all possessed a common feature—tall height, blue eyes, and handsome.

Virgil quizzed them on their birth years, and our heroes agreed that the early, nineteen-century never evolved to the glamour of the twentieth century. This strange group never knew the magic of American cinema. *Yet they sensed something different.*

"These people are simple and easily swayed," Virgil opined. *Good observation.* "Let's move on!"

As the hours went by, Dunstan met more pioneers in this particular region, but no one mirrored such a reaction. This bucolic, rural splendor evoked memories of Central America. They came across another town by a long dead railway line. In one bar, a motley colored group played cards. Others drank whiskey at the bar for an eternity. Many, however, sat, eating sandwiches and drinking coffee. All consisted of pioneers who had harsh lives. Every table was decorated with fresh flowers and tasteful knick knacks. On the walls featured replicas of record sized fish catches and prized hunting finds.

Ok, here it comes! How can I say it? "What can end this upside down society?" Dunstan mused, surveying the characters, which looked like stock characters in a western. In fact, Dunstan was passionate about Westerns. Legend has it; Jimmy Stuart wore the same hat in all the Westerns he acted in. As a matter of fact, Max still remembered the fight sequence between him and Gregory Peck in The Big Country, where the camera captured them as two, small figures fighting. In the background, the land was so vast and the characters came off as insignificant to the landscape.

There is no sense to this. "What is the meaning of life?" he lamented. "Is this all for nothing?"

"People are in hell because they cannot forgive themselves," Virgil replied. *Here he goes again with this nonsense.* "You seem to forget, in this world you will see many strange things." he added, looking off. *I've seen enough!*

Meanwhile, members of the locales discerned the fact that the heroes of this tale possessed no shadows. True to form, these entities viewed this phenomenon as an oddity, unique in these parts. Yet no one did anything. One personage raised his hat and stared at Dunstan, kicked a chair over, and ordered a drink.

"I'm Rudolph Velentino, who are you?"

I know you! "Max Dunstan."

That moment, the men then exchanged pleasantries and greetings.

Film buffs considered Valentino the first sex symbol of the silent film era. As the hours went by, in this strange land, Dunstan and Valentino spoke of American politics.

"Sounds like to me," Valentino stopped to grasp the present, political situation. "Borders don't mean anything anymore. The world is heading towards a set of uniform laws and a single world currency, or it would blow apart."

Outside they saw carriages from another era go by. All the kings, Queens, and tyrants of history performed in the holograms in the sky above.

As the night went, he met other strangers who regaled him with tales of war, or triumph. A silent, difficult to please Virgil found this episode rather dulled his senses and forever annoyed him. At the end of the evening, when they left the bar, they looked at the strange constellations in the night sky. Again, they stopped abruptly.

What is the matter now? "Why are we stopping?"

"You're still not ready." Virgil replied, with absolution. *Why not!* "Let not hate, no anger, or guilt, cloud your mind." *Here he goes again, filling my mind with nonsense. This is all so immaterial.*

Dunstan insisted that all his experiences have manifested a change within him. He argued he felt like a better person, a changed man. Eventually, Virgil just sighed and shook his head.

In a flash, they heard machine gun fire and the sounds of a black corvette that sped off from a local bank.

Right to bear arms! "See guns don't kill people. People kill people," Dunstan argued, making Virgil roll his eyes. *That's proof enough!*

Meanwhile, Virgil then breathed in and out. In a heartbeat, Max then noticed a change in his guide's facial features.

Now what! "What's the matter?" He felt a coldness rush through him. "What's happening? Is something happening again?" *This is never ending. Death ain't like in the movies— no one goes off into the white light, living happy ever after!*

Out of the blue, the ground moved them toward the bank doors, which opened. In minutes, they seemed to glide. *Better than an escalator.*

"Where are we going?" Dunstan entreated. "What is happening?"

Here it comes. This must be bad! "Let's see who was affected by your guilt?" Virgil conceded. *What is this man talking about!*

The men then glided past a bullet-ridden window. The ambulance had long since come and taken the victims to the hospital.

Dunstan saw the police placing the bank security guard into a body bag.

"Well," someone said aloud. "Insurance would never cover him anyhow." *You mean he could still be saved.*

They suddenly stepped into a vortex, where they saw several persons in an Emergency Room. A Hispanic male, age 21, and the father of two three year old children. The illegal alien had no health insurance. The lanky young man wore plain dark blue jeans and a nondescript hooded sweatshirt.

Right to bear arms! "If he had a gun, he would not be here," Dunstan mused.

"He was working several jobs to support his family because his father fell sick and could not work anymore," a mysterious voice replied. *Who was that?*

Virgil then went on to reveal how the now dying young man had dreams, but they got squandered because of Dunstan's vanity, greed, and stupidly. Like clockwork, the celebrity argued otherwise, but his protestations got cut short by Juan ending his life on the saying of the Lord's Prayer.

Sweet misery! "You put him here," a long dead mother accused him. "He would never go near drugs, guns, or criminal activity," she added.

This has to be nonsense. Complete garbage! "He entered the country illegally and took away an American's job," Dunstan argued. *That ought to tell them!*

"He would have been on a farm picking vegetables with other immigrants. No hardworking American would take this job!" Virgil thundered, silencing the screen legend.

Meanwhile, as Juan and the other wounded person in the ER room blurred, they all faded into a black background. In a skip of a beat, Virgil motioned for Dunstan to sit down, and engage in breathing activities. Again the guide repeated the warnings for the icon to avoid the vices of anger, hate, and guilt. As they breathed in and out, a warm energy covered them, taking the two a million miles away.

A mist lingered in this milieu. A short, dark, and solidly built Robert Blake came forward. "Beware what you see, yet do not believe," Blake warned. The actor then disappeared into the void.

"Strange bird in a strange tree," Virgil observed, shaking his head.

In a flash, Kelsey Grammer then emerged from the oblivion and scrutinized them, shaking his head. *What does he have to say?*

Grammer lost many family members to violence but somehow was drawn to the works of 'William Shakespeare' and spent two years at the prestigious Juilliard School. He then dove into Broadway with roles in "Macbeth" and "Othello." He joined the cast of "Cheers" in 1984.

Ok, this must be someone too! "Who is this now?" Dunstan ejaculated. The envoy shook his head. "What were you on earth?"

"An actor, a movie star, and loved by millions," the illusion replied. "I am nothing now," it affirmed, before disappearing. *Don't recall your face. Who is he!*

"Don't believe what you seen, nor hear," his guide warned.

"Whenever your wise friend says, ignore him," Grammer yelped, cackling.

Meanwhile, as this conversation took place, atomic bombs went off in the background.

"Where are you from?"

"America," it replied. *Such a suspicious character.*

"That damn Bush family has ruined our country," it added.

"What else do you know?" Dunstan begged, ignoring his glowering diplomat.

"They don't make movies the way they used to! Reality TV! Who would take *US* seriously in the world! This generation is being robbed of good entertainment!" the phantom raged.

"Give me Jimmy Cagney, instead of Jean Claude Van Damme."

You are preaching to the choir! "I agree with you!"

"I prefer Jimmy Stuart over Tom Hanks any day."

"They're both good!"

"Bull shit!" *This man is very bitchy.*

In the horizon above, a strange scene appeared from Dunstan's unconscious. A doctor stood over a nine-year-old child with a liver disease. She needed a liver transplant, or she would die. The father faced the physician, who scrutinized the clothes of the despairing parent.

"Do you have health insurance?"

"No we can't afford it!" the father muttered, sobbing.

"We can't serve you without coverage."

"Bastards!" the man screamed. "Jesus Christ! I have a son, my little girl, and another on the way! What am I supposed to do!" he fired back.

"Get some coverage!" the doctor replied. "We can't help you."

Meanwhile, Dunstan saw other visions of a grandfather selling his home to finance his grandchild's operation. Max looked at the victims being left in the hallway to die. An unwed mother used her humble wage at the grocery store to pay a man with a coat hanger to end her pregnancy. *So horrifying and gruesome, I had to look away.*

"You will see many strange things," Virgil muttered.

That's an understatement. "Where are we going now?"

"As you ascend, you descend." *More puzzles and mystery to the wicked?*

"Where are we going?"

"Nothing lasts forever." *Let's hope so.*

CHAPTER ELEVEN

Spheres opened up and enveloped the two into a sea of atoms and molecules, where the central sphere moved infinitely, but its nothingness, something devoid of time and space. In a flash, the middle sphere, a mere seed that grew into itself. It could not be expanded into whatever surrounded. This central sphere, nothing more than a living organism which fluctuated through birth, life, death, and reincarnation. But there remained an immortal essence of energy force, which continuously increased the magnitude of aliveness and consciousness. As time went on, this process led up to the self-creation of a bigger sphere of being. The final aim and purpose resulted in an act of self-creation that exceeded the mode of human thinking. *It certainly did so!*

The knowledge of these cosmic processes came to be imprinted in the minds of those who traveled these strange roads. But this knowledge and its laws also affected the basic structure of all forms of life which included man, animal, plant, planets, and the stars.

The rings of the universes resembled a magnetic field, or an aurora borealis, a kind of spectral orb. In its conventional state, the ultimate sphere contained a cloud, or field of light. *But the last sphere all words and symbols failed here. Reason failed. No words, or sounds, could be used to express the impossible.* Wiseman called the last sphere not only the gods of the universe, but the origin of the creator, nameless and unknown to most living beings. If it had a name, it represented the primary sound of all creation. This nameless being, a mere cloud of living, transparent light.

A light manifested in this sphere, where an energy field possessed a state of undifferentiated oneness. This signal that emitted a beam of light represented the completion of a cycle, where lower, level gods entered and returned from all directions. When these crude beams of energy grew, a million orders of the universe were sprung, giving life to a many worlds and other beings, yet to be born.

It had red-colored atomic fires of immense intensity. These seeds contained the foundations of the universes and all their forms of life. *Nothing like I had ever seen before!*

After its explosion, the dense state, broke open and released its life force. This force became basis of all life in the universe and galaxy itself. *This wasn't in the Bible!*

"You will see many strange things," Virgil muttered. *Sometimes it is best unexplained.*

"Where are we going now?" *This man and his Buddha like mind set when we mortals feel what we see!*

"As you ascend, you descend." *Mere words, all added to the list of double talk.*

"Where are we going?"

Here we go again! "Nothing lasts forever."

"Who are you again?" *More questions again?*

"Are you from the other side? Are you the man who created the world?" *Who knows maybe he has an actor's ego too.*

"Through vanity, greed, and stupidity this world sprung." *Told you so!*

Dunstan saw a headline blazing across the sky stating: Ten thousand Americans die each year from gun violence, due to insufficient health coverage.

This can't be so! "My god!" he lamented, holding his head. "What have I done!" he cried. *Maybe I had a part in it after all!*

"Hell is for those who can't forgive themselves," Virgil uttered, calmly, yet succinctly, a mere cloaked man.

"Take them away!" Dunstan begged. "Take them all away!" he said again. *Give me my peace. I deserve more!*

"Your creation." *This has to be one giant illusion.*

"Why don't they just go back where they came from?"

"It is not their time," Virgil replied." It *NEVER* was their time," it added. *I saw that coming too!*

In a skip of a beat one phantom glided forward, offering marijuana, which both men refused. *He should be ticketed.* "Has this always been the way?"

"You must bleed the blood of every victim. Feel the sorrow of every soul lost. For an eternity."

How about a true felt apology! "Why!" Dunstan cried. "I want you to take these people away. End it all!" he added. *Enough is enough.*

"Greed, vanity, and stupidity have created this place." *You said that before, many times before!*

Meanwhile, the noise of the crowd deafened him. Sunlight couldn't break through this heavy haze of smoke. Here Dunstan remembered the wrong that he did. He remembered standing before a pro-gun rally in view of a location where one school shooting had occurred. He felt regret, shame, and guilt. The frightening scene disappeared into the colorless background.

"Where are we? What has happened now?" *More things on the way?*

"Let greed, vanity, and guilt be left behind," Virgil said, sublimely.

"What guilt?" Dunstan argued. "I have no regret." *I am a better person. You should know this.*

Meanwhile, in the sky above they saw riots in the street. Another white cop was killed and a black youth placed into custody, leaving the streets filled with anger. Together the masses burned a flag and chanted Blood! Blood! Blood!

". . . The law-abiding citizen is entitled to own a rifle, pistol, or shotgun. The right, put simply, shall not be infringed . . ."

—Before the Senate Judiciary Committee 9/23/98

In time, they now beheld an ancient man-made structure perched on a rocky, infertile ground, where a beach once stood. A collection of wrecked ships sat in the background. A lone, cloaked figure was positioned before a dying fire. He forgot to stoke the embers to keep the flames alive. The man had thinned, lines now covered his face, but his pensive gaze lingered. Dunstan thought about his career, the people he met along the way, and all the people that he had touched. He never dreamed the day would come where it all would come back to him. He rolled into the fetal position and used an old army blanket to protect himself from the ever present cold. In the night sky, he saw Bill Gates, Warren Buffett, and Jacob John Astor dining together in the finest restaurants of their times, where famous writers, actors, and celebrities came to be at their beckon call. In the next table sat Marilyn Monroe, Bo Derek, and Cindy Crawford. All these forms continually shape shifted into whales and dolphins. This mirage made Max shake his head at the celestial phenomenon. The Native and other ancient cultures perceived the mammals as superior beings which possessed divine powers. These animals exuded graceful bodies, effortless movements, and healing energies for the sick.

Time felt it had stood still. Dunstan, however, continued to shake his head at the apparition. In his lifetime, Dunstan actually turned down a role to star with Monroe in the film "Let's make Love." He found Monroe's desire to look too perfect killed her. He heard that Monroe spent all her time in her Winnebago and away from the set, angering actors, directors, and producers. *Not for me!*

"What is it you seek?" Derek ventured.

What do you think! "I had a dream, or vision," he stuttered. *When will this end?*

"You are seeing days long forgotten," she replied, resembling a mammal from the discovery channel.

In the meantime, Bill Gates espied the one who had parted the Red Sea for movie audiences.

What the hell! "Who are you?" the shark demanded. "Did you just speak to me!" he added, flabbergasted. *Is this me, or does he have a great dentist?*

"You soon will know," Monroe interrupted.

Astor flagged a passing Waitress for the bill and Gates studied the lonely man by the fire.

"What do you want from me?" he asked. *Don't know?*

"I have nothing," Dunstan replied. "Please leave me in peace," he begged. *If you can call it that!*

"I hope my daughters on earth are not led astray to dwell here," Micro-soft muttered, mildly. *Who knows what will come of her?*

Mother Teresa then came from the void, concern etched all over her face. "There is a place for you to stay at the Inn," the phantom offered.

Another misery added to my suffering. Dunstan shook his head. "I'm fine by the fire here," he replied. "Thank you for asking though," he added.

The two continued their journey along a grayish region, where nothing had any taste, or sense of smell. In time, Religious figures passed by them. He nodded to Moses and gave the thumbs up to Abraham. A ghost manifested along the bleak roadside. The conversation went as follows:

"Who are you?"

Does it matter anymore! "Nobody."

"You have any food, or drink?"

Nothing! "No."

That moment, the ground shook and the earth groaned.

At least we know we won't fall into the ocean! "What happened?"

"Nothing happened," it replied. "It is the way it's always been." *More double talk.*

For the time being, a series of aftershocks and sulfur dioxide started rising from a portion of a collapsed road. Some have said through earthquakes the myth of Hades sprung.

"Purity."

What is he on! "What!"

"I wrote a book, offending many," it revealed.

"What was its name?"

"The Satanic Verses."

Gotcha! "Solomon Rushdie!" *What a character!*

In the late 80's the Ayatollah Khomeini declared a fatwa against him. Khomeini proclaimed the book to be an insult to the Islamic religion. Rushdie lived many years under police protection since that time. Since the Ayatollah's death he occasionally appeared in public but always kept a watchful eye for extremists.

"Who are you?'

Here it comes! "Max Dunstan."

"May you find what you are looking for," it offered. That moment, its form fading into the oblivion. *What a great exit. He would have made a great actor, or a politician.* In a flash, Rushdie reappeared and went to embrace Dunstan; instead the form stepped through the thespian. *What the devil!*

"Now you see the purity?" Virgil said, cryptically. "It is where all the sense of the self is no more." *More double talk!*

That evening, they walked along a terrace in France. Not a living soul could be seen for as long as the eyes could see.

"Whatever will be, will be," Dunstan suddenly said, somberly and with resignation. *I have no expectations.*

As they continued to walk along a narrow, cobble stone road, an oak tree suddenly appeared.

"This is forbidden fruit," a mysterious voice announced the bodiless. Dunstan and Virgil exchanged looks, but the voice continued. "Eat this and you will be truly damned."

"Welcome to the Garden of Eden!" Max joked. *I now wish.*

Meanwhile, as they moved slowly around this tree, three faceless spirits confronted them. One carried a goblet of blood, which it readily consumed. All of a sudden, its facial features returned. A careful, critical observer would detect the unnatural thinness of the former female. It went through a period of which it wasted away. It stood patiently revealing its face.

Now who do we have here? "Hello, I'm Sally Struthers."

She had no hair and had shriveled down in size. Best remembered for her role in 'All in the Family' and a long-time TV spokesperson for the Christian Children's Fund.

"Hi," she said. "How are you?"

"Fine," he answered. "How are you?"

What else can be said! "Where are we?" our adventurer asked.

Virgil then discreetly pointed out that they now occupied the land of the gluttons. *Sorry for her.* Like always, the actors exchanged pleasantries, but their conversation got drowned out by Gene Simmons belting out Macho Man, all before a group of overfed Americans. He wore a big bird costume, minus any facial disguise. Everyone tried to follow him in an exercise routine, but some fell over, clutching their chests and gasping for life. These manifestations came and went, as many did. *Such as life it is!* Out of the blue, another shade materialized. Its features obscured by a haze. Gradually, it then consumed a goblet of blood.

Who is this? "Please don't look at them in such a way," she begged.

In a skip of a beat, her facial features soon appeared, revealing Karin Carpenter.

Carpenter in the early 1970s won several Grammy Awards, embarked on a world tour, and landed her own TV variety series. Sometime in the early 80's she collapsed from a cardiac arrest and died. Nobody knew that Ms. Carpenter had suffered from anorexia. Ms. Carpenter now held an iced tea, which was her favorite drink. "You want a sip?"

"No thank you." *I'm good to go.*

"It's no problem."

"No, I am fine." *So very gracious.*

Meanwhile, others came forward, including fashion models. All ugly and wafer thin. Some known and unknown.

Ok, here it comes. "Who are they?"

"The vain," Virgil opined, shaking his head.

He pointed out at the known, the unknown, the celebrity, and even the conceited. The soldiers who mocked Iraqi prisoners on America's War on Terror also remained. Dunstan nodded at some celebrities, but frowned on others. John Belushi, Steve McQueen, Peter sellers, and Errol Flynn all shared a drink in a nearby patio. *What a party they had.*

"If you have something to say, get it off your chest!" someone challenged Dunstan, who frowned.

"What's up?" George Burns chimed, who walked arm in arm with his wife Gracie.

"It's all so clear!" Michael Jackson squealed. "It's as if the answers were there all along," he added, guiding his children hand and hand. *He's weirder in person then on the TV.* Dunstan then turned to Virgil and held his face. More faces passed by him.

"I don't know the meaning of life," James Dean admitted, manifesting. "All I know is what I see, or feel. Even that I am not certain of," he added. *Sounds like an interesting person!*

Virgil went on to argue that even a street beggar can be trapped in a vice of greed and be lost. Without warning, another tree appeared.

"Move on!"

What's up here? "Why!"

"This is the tree that drove man from paradise," he replied. "Be warned!" he added, ruefully. *Ok.*

CHAPTER TWELVE

A streak of light appeared in the sky. A pulsating object descended from the heavens and landed nearby. Unexpectedly, Virgil and Dunstan were both carried away by an anti-gravity field. When they entered the craft, the gravity field mechanism was initialized; placing them in a still state, as the ship went thought speed into the cosmos. Fossil fuels, fuel cells, or solar power, did not power this space ship. It was endowed not only by mental engines, but by vortex power. Some shiny robots continually passed through the hallway adjacent to them. The flying object was small from the outside, but as big as a Hollywood, movie studio. They heard a myriad of voices chatter through a series of electronic waves. Eventually, they then landed on a mysterious planet.

This planet's atmosphere paralleled a strong greenhouse effect. The surface level endured exceptionally humid, but wind patrolled the air above the clouds. It also possessed a hot surface, which was constantly bombarded with solar radiation.

Powerful winds roamed the cloud tops, but winds at the surface proved very slow, no more than several kilometers per hour. However, due to the high density of the atmosphere at the planet surface, even such mild winds wielded a significant amount of energy. The clouds primarily forged sulfur dioxide and sulfuric acid droplets, shielding the planet completely, obscuring any surface details to the human eye.

The axis was tilted, its orbit had slowed, and rotation came to be extremely slow. The planet had two major continent-like highlands on its surface, rising over vast plains. The northern highland had the upper mountains, close to two miles taller than Mount Everest. In the Southern Hemisphere existed a landmass the size of North America. Between these highlands possessed a number of broad depressions.

Impact craters filled the surface, which was recently covered with lava. This suggested that the surroundings underwent a major, catastrophic shift. It also had a weak magnetic field compared to other planets in the universe. At one time this planet had as much water as Earth, but a comet, or asteroid induced a catastrophe, changing the environment forever. The terrain also possessed steeper mountains, cliffs and other features.

NASA should hear about this. The gravity field mechanism released them, letting them being carried by countless, invisible hands, where they landed several football fields from the mysterious vessel.

In due course, the travelers stopped at the top of a volcano, where vapor rose in all directions. Oddly, the sound of voices sang in a great chorus which filled the air.

Ok, I have a question for him. "How do the gluttonous become so thin?" *Take that hot potato and play with it.*

As Virgil answered this question, he became animated. His eyes appeared to bulge. At one time, he actually tore his hair out. His physical reactions unnaturally contrasted with his quiet matter of fact behavioral patterns. "As an alcoholic drinks, he will never be drunk," he argued. He also referred to how a drug addict would also never get high; their pains would never be lessened, but get aggravated and accentuated. Suddenly, in an instant, this response got interrupted by a volcanic eruption. "Don't look down!" he admonished. "Keep walking!" he added. He didn't stop there, but continued. "I beg you to focus on the journey ahead not the one where you have come from," he pleaded.

Out of the blue, a lustful voice called out from behind the flames, inviting them to join the naked bodies. When they crossed through a moist ground, Madonna's "Like a Virgin" played to cheers and praise to the travelers for their fortitude. In time, legendary, Hollywood vixens came forward, all exposing themselves in threadbare outfits. In a nanosecond, Hugh Hefner manifested in his bathrobe.

Another red flag? "Again be weary of those in this region," Virgil warned. "They mustn't be taken seriously."

Again with this mentality! "Why?"

"They are not who they claim to be." *More weird talk!*

"He is just from the other side," Hefner ejaculated into a mike, announcing Dunstan's arrival. Scantily clad blonds were at his disposal, all dressed in revealing, and provocative outfits. *How would I explain this to my wife!* Some, however, stripped naked and covered themselves in sex wax. One even had a cobra resting on her shoulders. A fire-eater regaled all with his skills. Some applauded, others masturbated, but the remaining crowd amused themselves with alcohol and feasts that extended into infinity. The smell of feces and marijuana hung in the air. If one went further, they would enter the underworld's yearly gay pride parade which was then headed by Liberace.

"Greetings, sir!" Wayne Newton offered. "Please come near the fire. Tell us who you are and where you have come from," he added, smiling at an expected applause.

Barry White took the stage and Dunstan grabbed a beer. A lush orchestra played, as White laid down his big baritone voice. As White's performance went into full swing, the whole gathering stopped, as a group of groupies chased Lee Majors up a stairway, where they pounced on him. *What a bizarre scene.* "I am just from the other side," Dunstan said, suddenly.

This is quite surreal! "Who are you?"

"I am nobody." *Enough said!*

An hour of merriment must have passed. They praised him for his modesty and his successful career. After the song, Hugh Hefner took the mike, and introduced his collection of Playboy Bunnies, much to Dunstan's amazement and Virgil's disgust. This whole scenario unfolded in this outrageous, carnival-type atmosphere. Towards the end of the evening, Hefner introduced every female that ever served him as an employee. This spectacle left Dunstan speechified and his guide horrified. His past customers consisted of actors, producers, politicians, all watching and applauding Hefner for his brilliance. Dunstan nodded to many colleagues that passed before him.

Clark Gable and Cary Grant both joined the gathering. *What are they doing here?* "Such legends," he muttered, almost inaudible. "There will never be another like them," He added. As a matter of fact, Dunstan claimed himself a big fan of Cary Grant. What he would have done to star with Grant in "The Grass is Greener." He respected the fact that Grant took chances and did it within the rigid studio system, where others had failed. Dunstan remembered being at a party at the American ambassador's residence and bragged to his wife about British Prime Thatcher being his dinner-eating partner. His wife Lydia turned around and said she had just spent time with Cary Grant, leaving Max envious about his wife's luck in the seating arrangements at the Two Hundred Anniversary of the British American Alliance.

A great siren sounded, signaling that the planet's largest volcano had erupted. Meanwhile, screams and cries filled the air. Some vixens ran in terror and headed for cover, as the ground quaked and people fled. Virgil frantically motioned for Dunstan to hurry. Sulfur dioxide and hot air shot from the surface and the area waters boiled. Nature killed all that dwelt in this strange land. In the smash hit "Earthquake" Dunstan and Ava Gardner got sucked up in a gushing torrent. At least his character in that movie died a decent death. *In reality, eternal rest would evade me.*

Sooner or later, our wayward travelers then felt unseen energies lift them from this turmoil. The same anti-gravity field that had brought them carried them into the same holding area where robots scurried back and forth. Electronic voices rattled off orders and a myriad of modems sounded. The gravity field holder were initialized and our passengers remained in its mysterious embrace, as the craft launched into mind speed.

This journey will never end. Even in "Planet of the Apes", his character was offered a decent death scene while facing a thermal nuclear explosion. After a while, as the craft emitted a series of sonic booms, Dunstan smiled, and said, jokingly," "Here comes the pain!"

"Think nothing," Virgil replied. "Leave fear, hatred, and guilt behind you," he added, solemnly. *When will this man ever make sense?*

In due course, the vessel passed through the time continuum, leaving Dunstan to go into a deep sleep. In his successful, movie career, he learned to sleep on jets, limousines, and in the makeup chair. In this predicament, whenever he closed his eyes, the forces of creation denied him the comforts supplied by the sandman.

"What is your decision?" a voice asked, bluntly.

"Very well," another replied.

Out of the blue, long dead family members guided him into a river of flame, where he felt no pain, but a sense of peace and joy. "The high is coming and the sun will soon eclipse," another voice warned, fervently. *What did these spooks say?*

He then had a dream of a pro-gun rally, sometime after the massacre at Columbine in Littleton, Colorado. He remembered being interviewed by Michael Moore, who left the portrait of a slain little girl behind. He later had his assistant dispose this picture in the compactor.

"Why did you do it?" she asked, weakly. "Why did you allow me to die!" she cried, innocently. *I had no part in it, young lady. Your parents should take responsibility their actions, or lack of that, for that matter.*

Right on cue, he woke up with a start. The vessel had long since landed and disembarked its prized passengers, and disappeared into the cosmos, now a mere star in the cosmos. His mentor stood and stared blankly at the forest before them.

"You have now come to the end of the journey."

I should get this in writing. "This is the end?" *He must be joking.*

"There will be many endings and beginnings," it replied. "Such is life," it added, sighing. *Told you so.*

Chickadees sounded in the distance. At intervals, one could hear a lion roar, or a bear foraging for food. Canada Geese flew in formation above. They even visualized a bald eagle in a nest, feeding its young. Over time, a narrow boardwalk guided them heroes through this rain forest to the side of a river, where one could not only see their reflection, but catch sight of trout swimming in it too.

David Letterman Quote
Mack Dunstan admitted he had a drinking problem, and I said to myself, "Thank God this guy doesn't own any guns!"

He heard a voice singing on the other side. None other than Barbara Streisand, the only artist to achieve Billboard #1 albums in four decades, the '60s, '70s, '80s and '90s. In life he had a conversation with a director friend about Streisand.

"How was it to work with Barbara?"

"It wasn't that bad."

"Word around town was that she was difficult to work with?" *A very demanding woman!*

"No she wasn't that bad, considering it was the first film she directed." *Must have been a real bitch.*

This conversation actually occurred between Max and Will Wyler, director of "Ben-Hur" and "Funny Girl."

A gentle wind blew a sky blue cape. Opal colored pearls hung from a necklace. Her gown was encrusted with ornate jewelry. Her voice, a mere song bird in the night air. Her long, blond hair appeared so natural and alluring. Warm, loving energy came from her countenance. Dunstan never recollected Streisand being so sensuous and voluptuous, as she came to be now.

Must be an illusion. "Please come closer," he begged to Babs. Streisand sang a song that surprisingly brought tears to his eyes. *This can't be real! She never ever made me cry!*

"Why are you so surprised to see me?" she asked "No one lives forever," she added. *The underworld is obviously not big enough.*

In the fullness of time, they saw wild animals passing them, which caused them no harm. Many of those creatures originated from pre-historic times. Dunstan then turned to Virgil. "Is this Utopia? The Fountain of Youth?" he quizzed.

"I've never seen this place before," his mentor replied, pensively. "It has not been seen for many moons."

"Is this time distortion?" *More mystery?*

"I know not what you speak!" *He'll never give a straight argument. He is a real lawyer.*

Streisand continued to walk and sing along the riverside. Dunstan followed nearby. Just like that, Babs stopped and pointed to the sky.

A swarm of flying saucers passed by, followed by a set of Las Vegas dancers, who performed for a small audience down below. At the end of their show, they disappeared, unleashing a round of fireworks, as far as the eyes could see.

"Wait a minute," she said. "Did you see it?" she asked.

"No," he yelled, smiling. All of a sudden, in a sparkle, he saw a group of strangers who manifested in the sky above.

CHAPTER THIRTEEN

A smile beamed from one of the friendly faces. Fairy dust sparkled around her, as her hair flew in the wind. A long flowery cape flapped like a sail with a purple edge to its every fold. A motley colored night gown released a myriad of doves, as it beat in the wind. Her waist down hair curled naturally. A warm, kind energy came from her face—none other than J.K. Rowling. *I truly meet them all!* In media reports, Rowling admitted to having been a bit of a daydreamer as a child and began writing stories at the age of six.

One day, stuck on a delayed train for four hours between Manchester and London, she dreamt up a boy called Harry Potter. Years would pass and eventually she became a world famous, children's author.

At present, however, Rowling appeared dressed as a fairy godmother. The sun shone down at them directly, preventing a shadow from being cast.

"Do you feel guilt for the suffering you have caused?" she asked, bluntly. He remained stoic. *What can I say?* She, however, continued. "Do you have anything to say for yourself?" she quizzed. Still he remained silent. *What does she expect me to say?*

"In your journey, what have you learned?" she questioned him. "What appealed to you?" *I wouldn't know where to start. I am as human as the next guy!*

Excerpt of Mack Dunstan's Harvard Speech

Let me back up a little. About a year ago I became president of the National Rifle Association, which protects the right to keep and bear arms. I ran for office, I was elected, and now I serve . . . I serve as a moving target for the media who've called me everything from "ridiculous" and "duped" to a "brain-injured, senile, crazy old man." I know, I'm pretty old . . . but I sure Lord ain't senile.

As I have stood in the crosshairs of those who target Second Amendment freedoms, I've realized that firearms are not the only issue.

No, it's much, much bigger than that. I've come to understand that a cultural war is raging across our land, in which, with Orwellian fervor, certain acceptable thoughts and speech are mandated.

For example, I marched for civil rights with Dr. King in 1963—long before Hollywood found it fashionable. But when I told an audience last year that white pride is just as valid as black pride or red pride or anyone else's pride, they called me a racist.

I've worked with brilliantly talented homosexuals all my life. But when I told an audience that gay rights should extend no further than your rights or my rights, I was called a homophobe.

I served in World War II against the Axis powers. But during a speech, when I drew an analogy between singling out innocent Jews and singling out innocent gun owners, I was called an anti-Semite.

This can't be happening. There has to be a point to all this! How can it all be undone! All of a sudden he broke down and cried, shaking his head, and covering his face in despair. Dunstan felt a great sense of relief, which until that moment had been hidden under a façade. "My god, what have I done!" he lamented.

Good to get it off the chest and out in the open! "Your guilt is felt." *About damn time too!*

Out of the blue, he saw children of every color and creed surrounding Rowling. She had two at her feet and pointed to them, one black child, the other Hispanic.

"This is want and this is ignorance," she revealed. "These are the twelve year olds who killed each other, or were murdered by the bullies in the school yard. These are the children that went before their time," she added, making Dunstan go white and too upset to speak.

"What's done is done!" he replied. "I *can't go back to undo my damage,*" he begged. *This can't be so. This can't be real. Unimaginable!*

Across the stream, Streisand had been no more. When he closed his eyes, he could still see the children's eyes. When he bent to drink from the stream, his thirst never quenched. When he faced Rowling, the best-selling children's author no longer walked on the ground, but flew into a stream. When they landed by the beach, J.K tried to clean one of the children in the water, but the dirt would still remain. Suddenly, in a flash, he saw a strange specter of murder in the children's eyes. Each more gruesome then the other.

What is that? "Can I still save them from such a fate?"

"No," she replied. "Because they are already lost," she added.

Before you know it, he went blind. However, it didn't take long for his vision to return. In due course, a procession of children quietly exited into the oblivion. In a flash, in its place manifested a tree, which sprouted up to a great height.

"This is the tree of a good and evil," Virgil muttered, absentmindedly. *Maybe we can sell it on eBay!* Instead of a snake occupying the branches, there sat Heidi Fleiss. *Who is this?* An immense blood red cape flapped in the wind. Her waist long hair was dyed red to improve her appearance. She also wore a flame colored gown which illuminated. Occasionally loathsome bats flew from this gown, scaring all who were caught in her gaze. At the height of her infamy Fleiss was known as the Hollywood Madam. Meanwhile, at present, Andrea the Giant now assisted her to the ground.

Who could have dreamed up such a group of characters? "It is not his time," a mysterious voice said. *What is that?*

"He is here too soon," another added. *Who are they?*

As Fleiss made her way towards the two, a Las Vegas dance show manifested around them, complete with dancing girls. Dunstan, however, did not recognize the show tunes, or its singers. Instead, he fell into a deep sleep.

"Wake up!" one voice urged. *Who are these people! These things spring from the subconscious!*

"Your journey is not over," another said. "It is has only begun," it added, cackling.

Sooner or later, Dunstan stirred and he realized the absence of Rowling. In her place Ms. Fleiss looked on.

"Where is your friend?" he asked aloud.

Some children remained and sat before the former, Hollywood Madam, listening to the pimp read the next Harry Potter book. As she uttered the words aloud, she looked at Dunstan. He saw a twinkle in her eyes.

Lightening filled the sky and thunder rolled. In such a scene, an explosion hit outside, causing a tree to crash.

"Protect the children," an elf like creature cried. *What is that!*

"Save them from the madness of it all!" a midget howled. *Who is that!*

"Oh! The vanity of it all!" a madman raved, before succumbing to insanity. *Agreed!*

The earth quaked and a piece of the ground opened up, sending bodies falling down below. When the figures scrambled to their feet, they faced Ms. Fleiss and the Giant. "Your time is not yet come," she sighed. "Your journey is not yet begun," she added.

They keep saying this? "What is the meaning of this upside down world!" he entreated, angrily. *What is the point of it all! There is a point to this . . . has to be!*

"I don't know what you speak."

More weird talk! "Where do we go from here?"

"Let all hatred, anger, and guilt be clear from you," she replied.

This again! "How!"

"Let it all go!"

Easier said than done. "How!"

"Your time will come soon," the form responded. "Your journey will yet start," it added. *If it has not already!*

After a while, an eclipse happened. He looked to Ms. Fleiss, whose beauty radiated. The Giant just looked on. Soon enough, he found himself bathing in water, where the forces of nature all weighed in on him, forcing him to free his heavy mind. Max didn't fight it and felt the warm energy, or so he thought.

I have unquestionably been killed in more films than any leading actor in the history of the movies. I just now counted it up: fifteen times, only once peacefully in bed. Make a note of that . . . it may appear in the test.

Mack Dunstan, In the Arena, an Autobiography.

Dunstan then saw Fleiss, her eyes fixed intently on the sun. He imitated her and found himself on a mountaintop, perplexed at the specter of the fire at the very top of this world. *What have I done to land up in such a place? How did it get here!* In a flash, the particles shone in the sun's rays, revealing a great staircase descending from the sky. He even caught sight of sun worshippers above. *They have a way to go!* The sun's ethereal rays shone on him, changing him into a radiating being where atoms and molecules not only flew through him, but took him along a solar wind. *I must be on drugs!* In time, this engulfed him into a maelstrom. In the end, he saw family members and friends, who had long since died. *Here again*! In a jiffy, Fleiss conspicuously placed herself beside him.

"You have only yourself to blame for coming before your time," she told him, gently. *You'll make a believer out of me yet*! That moment, they felt a tremor. "You may still think you are alive and on earth, but you are wrong."

Is that so? "What can I do?"

"Let go of all the hate, the anger, and guilt," she exclaimed. "Break away from the self," she added. *I knew I had it in me!*

They moved across an ocean of life immersed in fire. At this time, she taught Dunstan on the rational that the afterlife reflected a person's conscience.

"If you are a money lender, a debtor's prison will be your punishment," she said. *That's why it is good to go showbiz!*

At once, they sailed through the Milky Way on an energy sphere, where he saw a series of holographic images of civilizations rising and falling. Dunstan saw all the descendants of all the empires, kingdoms, and civilizations burning in the fire. He saw drunkards drinking ale, yet devoid of any pleasures. Fleiss then turned to Dunstan. She argued how a person must be spiritually prepared for the Lands of the Dead. As they flew through space, he saw Mars, Venus, Jupiter, and the moon Titan, all complete with mining colonies from another solar system. They flew by a myriad of energy spheres, where he could hear the sound of fire engines sounding, ambulances racing by, modems going off, and fax machines screaming.

"Time Distortion?" he speculated. *Who would ever think?*

"The universe is a living organism and man is a mere manifestation," the Hollywood Madam spoke. "When the universe thinks, man appears. When a man dies, it should be obvious that the universe ceased to think about the said individual," she added, but she still continued. "If a man cannot let go of the land he owned, the wealth he had, then he will burn with others, until he lets go of the self," she added. *That would make a great sci fi film too!*

"What about heaven?" *Here it comes!*

"Heaven is much a prison as hell." *Sounds odd but interesting. She could still have a hidden agenda!*

Meanwhile, they passed through many solar systems, which teamed with life.

"The more I know, the less I know," he admitted. "Where is Earth? *She's the boss and in charge.* The pimp pointed to the small dot behind them.

"That is where tyrants raged, kings ruled, and soldiers fought and died," she replied.

"Incredible." *Through the good book, you can STILL get frequent flier points to the most exotic locales too!*

"Now you truly see Earth is not the center of the galaxy."

Definitely no argument from me! "The more I know, the less I know," he replied. "I know nothing," he added. *I was just an actor who said his lines.*

"Let go of the self, the pleasures, and pains," she encouraged. "Embrace the interconnectedness of the universe," she added. *Within reason I will.*

In space he saw phantoms and ghosts alone, or in strange, flying machines.

"They are real." *Or are they!*

"Are they?" *Do they have agent representation?*

"They once were, but now are forgotten," she explained. *And so we all will join them one day. If not already!*

Out of the blue, a rowboat drifted by and Dunstan waved at its passengers and they returned a friendly salute. *They don't have a safety vest or a lake to sail in. They can get a fine for that!*

What the jumping! "Who are you?" he screamed, making a suddenly appearing Virgil wince. *This man should announce himself before popping up like that.*

In a flash, she telepathed the screen legend, raising his kundalini, inducing an intoxicating flow of energy to seize his senses.

"Don't fight it," the Madam imparted. "It will only be hard on yourself," she added. Dunstan saw space ships piloted by life forms, both living and dead. In time, flying saucers traveled by them, causing him to jump. Who knows how long had passed. Maybe a day, or even a life time. He found himself absorbed with the sense of confronting infinity. "A man who dies and cannot let go of his possessions or self, creates his own hell," the Madam uttered. "Heaven is much a prison, as hell," she added. Dunstan scratched his head and buried his face in his hands. *Maybe this can be so!* Fleiss fixed eyes with Dunstan and sighed. "I see your plight."

"What can I do?" *Here it comes. Give me the bad news, Doctor!*

"Become desireless." *What the devil is she talking about?*

CHAPTER FOURTEEN

Dunstan laughed about the sheer thought of dying and facing a Hollywood Madam in the afterlife. "That's the talk which would put you out of the business," he joked.

"You must let go of your homes, the wealth, and where you come from, and embrace infinity," she replied, enthusiastically. *This is out of this world.*

This celebrity couldn't shake the images of those who died because of his promotion of the weapon's industry. He waved his hand in a dismissive gesture. "My God!" he cried. "What have I done!" he beat his chest. *How can I undo it all when the fight has been over this far!*

"Let it all go!" she countered.

"This is not for real!" he argued. "You are not for real!" he screamed at the illusion, which went pale. In a flicker of an eye, he tried to punch her, but his fists went right through her, making him recoil.

All of a sudden, they broke into a huge passionate kiss. He felt the sensation of a deep, open mouth kiss, and this pulled them close together. He seized her supple breasts. So sudden it began, she wiggled her way out of his grasp, where he faced a firm slap. *I believe that one!*

"I'm not that type of girl!" she shrieked. *Please don't tell my wife!*

The movie actor took a breath and smiled. "That kiss was the stuff of legends," he replied, wryly. *I suppose she knew that was coming.*

Very soon, a craft came from the cosmos, landed, and fired a warm, illuminating energy, lifting the pair up. *This is never ending! Aliens seem to like me*! Moments later, they then flew off in another direction, a million miles away. In time, they saw the inhabitants of an alien planet that moved in all directions. Some entities hunted and gathered. Others, however, went about their chores and business.

No wonder NASA didn't send a probe here, he mused, sardonically. *Would have costed millions!*

"The universe is a living organism. Whenever it thinks, man appears," she replied. *Here we go again.*

"When did you become so wise, Ms. Fleiss?" he teased. *In fact, I remember someone connected with her complained how manipulative she was, or is?*

"I know not what you speak," she retorted, indignantly. *Queen of double talk*! She, however, did continue to speak. "Let go of all your hate, anger, and guilt. Open your mind to the infinite," she exclaimed. *Whatever happened to her must have manifested such a mental change, or did it?*

"When did you see the light?" *If she still does exist.*

"I know not what you speak?'

A thousand souls with torches flew beside them, guiding them through the myriad of spheres, whose existence would baffle the minds of the entire world's present intelligentsia. *Ok, explain this!* Suddenly she vanished. *How convenient!*

Where did she go? "Hey! he cried. *What happened to her?* He looked around wildly.

In a split second, she reappeared. "You really have learned nothing from me. Haven't you?" she quizzed.

Staying in one spot. "I am all ears!"

"You seem confused."

"No I understand." *Not anymore.*

"Death is a mirror that reflects man. If a man is holding any hate, anger, or guilt, he will create his own hell and burn, until he is free from all such vices," she spoke.

Can this be possible? "Such vices are prisons?" he questioned the entity.

"Essentially, pain releases those of their earthly worries and burdens," she replied. *How can this be applied to reality? Is there a hidden agenda here?*

In the twinkling of an eye, Dunstan, Fleiss, and the ever present Virgil all rose upwards into a world of spheres. In time, joyful faces and flickering lights welcomed them. Dust particles moved in the solar winds and lights flickered. He saw no clouds, or rain. A great light glided over them.

"Who are you?" *This must be heaven, but we are yet to officially arrive.*

"I was a long lived person on planet earth," a voice replied. "We met at the Pentagon many times," it added, following a silence.

I'll hazard a guess. "Mr. Smith." *Gotcha!*

"I am the spirit formally known as John Smith."

In the 50's and 60's, Dunstan worked closely with future Governor and President Ronald Reagen, who then became president of the Screen Actors Guild.

Through Reagen, Dunstan met and had dealings with JFK, Vice President Johnson, speaker of the house, and a myriad of senators. In that era of his life, Washington used Max as a special emissary on cross-cultural missions. They sent him to Nigeria, where Dunstan met and befriended Mr. Smith of the US State Department.

Smith first sent Dunstan to Australia, New Zealand, Rangoon, and Bangkok to promote American cultural in the world's far off places. Dunstan used this association through the State Department to support American troops in all parts of the planet. When the USSR collapsed, Smith sent Dunstan to promote Western culture. He also sent the famed actor to China to perform at the People's Art Theatre. Eventually, the State Department declared these cross culture missions a success. A connection with Smith actually tried to motivate Dunstan to run for the senate in the early 70's. Dunstan's love, however, rested with the stage and cinema. He just loved to act. When Dunstan's conservative views clashed with Hollywood liberals, Smith encouraged Dunstan to quit acting and become the president of the National Rifle Association. People rarely associated the weapon's industry with the State Department, the CIA, or the world's billionaires.

It has been such a long time. "What happened to you, sir?"

"If I could not have been born, I would have done so."

What has gotten into his head? If it is him at all! "Why?" *How can you say such a things. Look at your accomplishments.*

"We secret society types decided who would be President and who qualified to be elected," it lamented. "And if I could not have been, I would."

This sounds crazy! "How long have you been here?"

"I have been here an eternity and will be here forever." *Why!* That instant, Smith's light disappeared and Osama Bin Laden and Saddam Hussein came in his place. Out of the blue, his fire lighted the way for other infamous individuals. They included Hitler, Napoleon, and Joseph Stalin. They waved to Dunstan, who returned them the middle finger. Such a gesture induced the dictators to become indignant.

Neville Chamberlain missed his chance. "I wish I can live forever," Dunstan murmured. *Such a pipe dream too.*

"All things come and go," a mysterious voice replied. "All things come and go," it repeated, but this time with a sarcastic laugh. *Who was that?*

"I know nothing lasts forever," another voice said. *Who, or what, was that?*

In the meantime, Saddam's sister came forward from the void. She told her story and ended her meeting with a cryptic prophecy.

"America will fall," she volunteered.

"What do you mean?" the American challenged her.

"Great men of finance gave Saddam wealth beyond his dreams of avarice," she offered. "They also bestowed upon him his troops the best arms and training. They supplied him with weapons, whose companies are listed on Wall Street itself," she added.

How can this be? "Are you talking about Saddam, or Bin Laden?" he interrupted, haphazardly. *What is she getting at?*

"When he turned against them, the men of finance made more money," it admitted.

"Who are you talking about again!" he screamed. *This sounds like nonsense.*

"For their treachery, nuclear clouds will return the earth to fire, whence it came," it spoke, sublimely.

What is going on here! "Can the future be changed!" *This can't be so.*

"Man never was," it replied, cryptically again. "Man never was at all. You really never were at all," it added. *Whose opinion is this . . . are you for real!*

"What do you mean by that?" *What is this?*

"I know not what you speak." *More mumble jumble and double talk.*

"Will the world end!" *This must be it.*
"No!"
"Why!"
"It is a forever spirit." *These guys are really from another planet.*

They saw many spheres pass through them. The long dead smiled at them, but others sneered. Kings, lawyers, and criminals saw them travel through their spheres, mere ghosts wandering through the time continuum. They regarded some souls rise from the masses in triumph and disappear into a crack of light into the spatial landscape. Today, technology could not even detect the existence of such other worlds, its people's, or species. Meanwhile, the strange constellations of the stars, its formation, many sights, and wonders awed the wayfarers. The beings and their brilliance humbled the heroes. The continuous radiance of their pyramids, its structures, and temples emitted the emergence and flight of clouds. In time, Dunstan's jaw just dropped in awe of such proceedings. Virgil and Ms. Fleiss looked on nonchalantly. These creatures not only possessed brilliance, but an art and skill beyond earthman's mode of understanding and invention. They saw blissful beings live in harmony. Classical music emanated from their lips, they possessed diamonds as their currency, and communication came as telepathic. They lived and dwelt according to the laws of the universe. In the meantime, Dunstan took a drink from a nearby goblet and the wine he consumed filled him with peace and wisdom.

As time went on, their faces grew into the great thinkers and Wiseman of our time. *Obviously a narcotic.* Ghandi came forward, a myriad of lights with forever, changing faces. Torches were affixed to the walls, lighting the gathering. Meanwhile, Dunstan stared into such fire and saw an age that had come and gone. He saw asteroids and comets crashing into the earth, ending each successive civilization, ushering in another period, all of which had been long forgotten in the history of life, where all roads to the past, present, and future.

The outward lines of a person manifested, making a myriad of spheres go blood red. It sharpened the lights and sounds of such images, almost obliterating Dunstan and the others around him. Great flying machines, both singular and connected to other magical forms illuminated those watching. The surrounding scene was ever changing, everlasting, and self-creating. Even the most arrogant egocentric and narcissistic mortal would be humbled in such far off exotic lands and locales. Infinite chains of circles of souls shone in the cosmos, extending from the remote past, to the present and unimaginable future. Very soon, Dunstan discerned painted faces, as far as the eyes could see.

He saw lifetimes yet to come. As a matter of fact, when he thought of a name, a face flashed across the sky. A single world soul appeared before them. That instant, it sang a song, unknown to mortals. It shone a celestial ray on him, penetrating his innermost being. He saw times and places lost in the history of time. Bob Dylan materialized and sang a song. Others also came forward too.

"Look into my eyes," the world soul implored the Lilliputians. *This man is the big guy!* Dunstan found himself feeling anger, hate, and guilt all the same time. At times he thought he felt lost in the sensations of madness. Mountains, volcanoes, and other spirits became grotesque and hideous.

The owlish faces of Thomas Edison and Benjamin Franklin came forward, followed by Ghandi, Winston

Churchill, Martin Luther King, and Mother Teresa. They not only hooted a hello to each other, but their wisdom shone through the ages. In a flash, a myriad of lights, both big, and small ascended and descended in all directions. A light flashed forward, stopping in front of Dunstan. In its fire, he discerned their faces—the musicians, who played their instruments when the Titanic went to the bottom of the Atlantic. *Good Lord! Poor souls indeed!*

"Truth is like the treasures of a long lost, Spanish galleon," the world soul said, its voice all sounding echoes throughout the lands and beings of the underworld. "Sometimes it is covered by the ocean sands, other times it is not," it added. *This man knows how to make a point.*

Lightening flashed and thunder sounded. Another light descended from the constellations. He looked into this grand mystery and saw the image of Bono, who sported goggle-like sunglasses. Dunstan was in awe with this experience and his surroundings. He looked to Ms. Fleiss for an explanation, or wise council, but she met him with a warm smile. Meanwhile, a meteorite burned through this strange world's atmosphere. It burned into a flickering light, which fired toward our hero and stopped. A famous face returned his gaze, none other than James Stewart.

Stewart's "aw shucks" demeanor served him well as the good guy, the shy guy or the nice guy in films. One of Dunstan's warmest memories of Jimmy Stuart came when Stuart wished him well hours before Susan Hayward read out Dunstan's name in the best actor category at the 1960 Academy Awards. Max remembered kissing his wife, giving a short speech and savoring his win, as he read the next day's LA Times.

The spheres rotated around them and space sprung its priceless jewels. On one passing asteroid sat the remains of a ruined abbey. Fleiss looked to the Hollywood legend and said, majestically: "Remember in your heart," she continued. "Man creates his own hell. And heaven is much as a prison as hell," she offered, before clasping her hands together.

Souls and flying machines from ancient times circled over them, making this locale both surreal and exotic. Out of the blue, a formation of flying saucers entered the solar system. They led a great shuttle, which some heralded as the largest and fastest craft in the galaxy. Its brightness caused blinding in all who beheld its rays. As it descended, the earth and the heavens trembled. When it landed every being shook in the universe. A great ramp descended from the vessel. Twinkling figures manifested in this environ.

Buddha, Allah, Christ, and the Prophet Mohammed sublimely strode off the vehicle, as it shone a gentle luminance. *Incredible! What a sight to behold!*

CHAPTER FIFTEEN

"What a sight!" Dunstan exclaimed. "Incredible!" he added.

"Here they come!" Fleiss cried. *Obviously an understatement.*

"What!" another yelled.

"Just wait!" someone replied. *Must be the long lost brother of Jesus Christ!*

In the meantime, the saucers hovered over the ground. There the wise men remained in suspended animation for an eternity. Fleiss now found herself weighing the pros and consequences of imparting knowledge into the late actor. Dunstan seemed to know her feelings and nodded, giving her the thumbs up signal. As more lights descended from the cosmos, one such light emerged and stopped before them.

This can't be so! "My gawd! You're Woody Allan!" Dunstan roared. "I love your work to death!" he added, excitedly.

The famous director stared at his old colleague and scratched his head. Allen retreated into a mystic like haze and bounced back re-invigorated.

The most prolific American director of his generation, who has written, directed, and starred in a film just about every year since 1969.

"I am just a star in the Milky Way," the comedian revealed, philosophically. *Another understatement.*

"Now that you are dead, do you still consider yourself an atheist?"

I'm listening! "No! I am still an atheist!" the filmmaker replied.

"An atheist in heaven?"

"Who's the director here?" *No argument from me!*

That moment, Virgil stepped forward. "Mr. Allan, you were divine in Bananas," the poet admitted. "I am a fan!" he added, enthusiastically. *The underworlds' first groupie!* This comment was met with indifferent and stunned silence.

"I have had better work," the filmmaker deadpanned. *I am sure you have.*

Meanwhile, Dunstan pointed to the space ships complete with wise men of all the ages. "Explain them!" he ordered, almost laughing.

"Their auditioning for an off Broadway Play," Allan replied, causing the specters around him to erupt into laughter. *Good to see he's still got his sense of humor!* The newly dead bowed to everyone who saluted this gesture. He now rested his attention on Mr. Allan. "As for you," he said, almost not knowing what to say. He never expected to meet this noted, comic master in such a place. "Have you ever considered seeing the psychiatrist in Hades?" he muttered, not knowing what would happen next. He had tried to think of a memorable response to the best in the business, but he wished to learn the great man's answer.

"Insurance won't cover it," the director quipped. *Good answer.*

Another light emerged from behind a low-lying hill. All of a sudden, it dove and stopped abruptly. That moment, motivational guru Anthony Robbins introduced himself and the men exchanged pleasantries. "You're the author of Awaken the Giant within!" Dunstan ejaculated. *I read that, I think.*

"Mr. Dunstan, what you need is confidence. You need to take control," he advised. *Sounds like a plan!*

"How can that help me in the land of the dead?"

"What you really need to do is *VISUALIZE* yourself using your talents in a positive, productive way," Robbins replied.

I need more than just that! "How!"

"Formulate a plan and put it into action!" it responded. ""Whatever your mind can conceive and believe it *CAN* achieve," he added.

"Did you make up that great quote?"

"Napoleon Hill," it answered. *Well-read too!*

Without warning, Frank Sinatra and the Rat Pack manifested and began to perform. Moses had a faint recollection of stopping a drunken Dean Martin from making a fool of himself performing at one of Reagan's inauguration, but that happened in the past. *Let's let sleeping dogs lie.*

Dunstan could now see the mysteries of the universe that came alive in its naked detail. Lydia, his wife, came forward dressed in a wedding dress. Max remembered their nuptials in a twinkle in the eye. During WWII, the future movie and television star underwent basic training. He asked for his wife's hand in marriage, she said yes, and he went out to buy her a wedding ring. As they walked along a street, they came across Grace Methodist Church. They entered the building, sought, and found a minister. They wanted to get married immediately. Dunstan even offered him money, but the Minister shook his head, adamantly.

"Not from a soldier," the priest uttered. That moment, the two got married.

In a jiffy, he realized he couldn't see his wife, or his guide, Virgil, or Ms. Fleiss.

What has happened! "Your physical eyes are no more," a voice said. "Your third eye is opened," it added

Where am I now? "I do feel a sense of guilt for what I said and done," Dunstan muttered. *I hope they can see how genuine this feeling is.*

"Why did you do what you did?" another voice quizzed him.

"Hollywood blacklisted me for my right wing views," he whispered. *Time to tell them where the bodies are buried.*

"So instead of fading graciously into obscurity, you remained active in the NRA," it assumed.

Well said. "Exactly," he replied. "I have their blood money and a guilty conscience, and they have theirs to live with too," he added, ruefully. In a flash, lightening filled the darkness.

"They made me into a billionaire," he revealed. *And some.*

"This illusion ended when you entered the lands of the forever sleep," it interjected, lustfully.

"Alzheimer's was my Achilles heel," Dunstan mused, sighing. *It'll get you sooner, or later.*

"What is your choice now?"

"To go back and undo my damage."

"The world you knew is no more."

"What do you mean by that?" *More weird talk. These spooks are incorrigible.*

They saw a myriad of images of earth and a news report of a great plague killing billions and concerns of Washington invading Beijing. In time, a faded video footage revealed future US President Arnold Schwarzenegger ordering that the stockpile of nuclear weapons concealed in the Midwest to be detonated. This conflagration induced earth to flare up in the cosmos. *Who would ever think? What got in his mind?*

Dunstan learned more. The news went as follows: in the course of this Third World War, which came sooner than anticipated, one billion human beings were killed and two billion were crippled and wounded. The nuclear fallout damaged the hereditary core of the race and civilization disappeared within a few generations. As a matter of fact, at the height of the Cold War, one trillion dollars a year were spent on hiring half the world's scientists to design and build bombs. When the Cold War ended, America had a stockpile of nuclear and biological weapons; enough bacteriological warfare available to annihilate the entire human races some five hundred times over. Even enough resources of chemical warfare to kill every single human being on earth some twenty five times over. The combined might of the world's nuclear and chemical arsenals killed the topsoil for generations to come, which ended life on earth forever.

This can't be happening. Wasn't Schwarzenegger an environmentalist?! This can't be so! This has to be a trick, but who, or what, could have such a hidden agenda? Only time will tell! Dunstan couldn't believe an action star would end humanity. At this time in his journey, a blinding light obscured the two; a solar wind took their souls away. *Here we go again!* An eclipse even occurred. Some faces went flush and tightened. "Schwarzenegger was elected American President," the dead man mused. *This can't be possible.*

"An amendment to the Constitution was passed and it allowed a foreign-born citizen to run for President," someone said. "Arnold Schwarzenegger was elected in 2012."

"Really!" *What made him do such a thing?*

That instant, outspoken actress and activist Jeannie Garafalo descended in the image of a Wood Pecker from the sky. "Hollywood has lost its pioneering spirit!" she cried. "Bottom line rules the roast. It's all who knows who. Everybody knows somebody, but they don't know who the hell they are themselves!" she added. *Test audience!*

As the clouds opened up and snow fell on the lands, the eclipse continued. "Don't look down," Fleiss warned. "Or the sight will surely kill you." As the astronomical phenomenon had begun, it soon ended. "Remember the universe is a living organism. When the universe thinks, man appears," Fleiss revealed.

In the twinkling of an eye, he saw a great canyon emerging in the sky.

"Look at the black hole," he marveled. "It is a gate way to another dimension," he added.

Fleiss' eyes began to glow and Dunstan noticed it.

"What is it!" he begged.

"The mind itself is a threshold to a whole new society," she muttered. Many spheres passed over them, some followed by strange, exotic flying machines. "Many levels of different realities await exploration and adventure." So w*hen again did she become so wise?*

"How do I make it there and come back?'

"No anger, no hate, or guilt must be buried in your heart," she said, firmly and succinctly.

Out of the blue, an invisible orchestra began to play them the theme song to 'Chariots of Fire', causing Dunstan to frown. *Why not Bach, or Mozart?* A great fireworks display then filled the sky. "Just like the 4th of July!" he mused. *Or so I thought. Could still be a trick from some yet unknown source!*

A red dot flashed in Fleiss' eyes.

"You have a question?" she asked. "Don't be shy," she coaxed. *I never knew of her to be psychic—what a lady*!

"How did the ancient Venusians or Martians seed life on Earth?" he asked, wryly. *Here it comes.*

"They injected a genetically created sperm into a group of earthborn chimpanzees and watched them travel in four directions," she replied.

"Where did they go?"

"Asia, Africa, Middle East, and India."

No Garden of Eden, or Snake? "Why not just have settlements on Earth?"

"It would take millions of years for an alien species to adapt to all the diseases on your home planet." *Far out*!

Furthermore, Dunstan speculated on the possibility of NASA sending a manned mission to an earthlike planet but Fleiss dismissed this realization as improbable and boldly predicted that if an earthborn man landed on another planet, disease would overtake him, as viruses doomed European explorers in the New World. *That's right, science has all the answers.*

Wild! "So who built the pyramids?" Dunstan quizzed the Hollywood Madam. *So explain that.*

"Man was genetically created to build the pyramids."

That wasn't in the Old Testament, or in the other section. "So an alien civilization did not build the pyramids?"

"Exactly."

"All our religions?"

"Man was genetically created to form customs, traditions, systems of thought, and religion." *Imagine the outrage she would cause on American television. They all would call her a loon but Ms. Fleiss would have quite a following.*

CHAPTER SIXTEEN

The Ninth Circle of light disappeared from their view. Dunstan found he and others again covered with particle beams which emanated from the cosmos onto the ground, and underworld. *This feels a lot better than it looks!*

"Remember the universe is a living organism. The stars, the star systems, the moons, and the planets are all part of the universal mind and we are the universal idea," she said, sublimely. *Here we go again! I should have seen this coming. She's a lunatic!*

In the meantime, the new light shone and a great wind blew from the east. He sensed the answers he sought had existed all along and saw a stream that flowed by him. He bent over, washed his face with the water, and even drank it. The cinema star saw the Earth before man appeared, the trees tall as skyscrapers and pre-historic creatures populated and inhabited its picturesque landscapes.

What an experience! "Look!" she regarded. "The earth is a forever spirit," she exclaimed. *That weird talk again.*

That instant, a grand holographic image appeared in the clouds, showing him a brief documentary on the rise and fall of ancient civilizations. *This can't be produced by Michael Moore!*

Princes, Kings, warriors, and world conquerors all appeared and disappeared, allowing him to see civilization after civilization rise and fall. Most of their ages were obliterated from memory, due to a celestial object hitting the earth, ending one age and beginning another. In time, this information program also featured the nuclear destruction of Modern Western Civilization.

"Hopefully the men of the future are wiser than their forebears," a mysterious voice said, its source unknown. *She must pay a pretty penny for her handlers.* These well spoken words left Dunstan deep in thought; inwardly debating the knowledge the forces of nature had imparted him. *Maybe I am crazy!* Out of the blue, his wife and children manifested before the thinking man. *Hello!* Meanwhile, a great army of flying saucers passed through the Milky Way. The infinite amount of energy of the universe radiated through him, everyone, and everything. *This is infectious!*

"When the universe thinks, man appears," another voice whispered. *This again. When will this all end, a mere nightmare!* Meanwhile, Fleiss' beauty glowed as fresh as the sunlight.

"Are you saying space itself is god?" Dunstan asked the entity. *This rational is the stuff of legend.*

"Everyone and everything is one," it replied. "There are no divisions," it added. *You can start a cult with that line of thinking, but will you make any money at it is the question?*

The radiance of the cosmos penetrated as deep as possible. He saw a great energy field, which manifested. Its volume would burn a mere mortal, a great being and a world soul. All of a sudden, filmmaker Michael Moore appeared. *The enemy!* Shining stars covered this images' cape, the robe sublime, his features proud, and serine. A scepter shone from one of his sturdy hands. This wizard ruled this environ, as in life his name had been known all through the lands. *He can't be behind this production!*

How can I start this one? I need a line here . . . line! Line! "Great Spirit!" Dunstan said aloud, falling down to the ground. *This will never make the trade papers any hoot*!

"It is the source for all thoughts and actions," Fleiss remarked. *You have quite a team*!

At once, Dunstan begged for grace and forgiveness. A light shone on the actor. His clothes burned free, but the omnipotent light obscured his shame.

Moore gestured and warned his former foe to not avoid the light. The Hollywood legend felt the wisdom of the ages permeate his whole being, a raw mental energy. He experienced the sensations felt only by wise men and mystics in the state of the super conscious levels. If he had avoided this light, the force of nature would condemn him, like many others, who forever roamed the lands of the dead.

O what a feeling! Wish it would never end! "Hang on!" Moore screamed. That moment, on a body of blazing light, they returned.

"Man creates his own hell, where he tortures himself," Virgil said, sublimely. "All hidden lies and violence become visible. Pain is endured when you are forced to face yourself, who you are, what you made of yourself, and who you could be," it added, stoically.

This can't be who I'm thinking it is! "What man does not know, he calls evil," it continued. "Man superimposes his hallucinations of Satan over creation, out of stupidly and ignorance of the universe and cosmos itself," it spoke.

Virgil spoke at length. He even argued that liberation from the underworld came through knowledge and precise action. The soul rose from torture, pain, and suffering by ceasing to think. Hence, the human mind which superimposed its reality. Thus ceasing the mind obliterated the hallucination of the other side. As a matter of fact, he encouraged Dunstan to meditate on the white light and this would free him from the torment. Only through such a practice, one would enter the path of rebirth. *Sounds like Buddhism.* Meanwhile, in this milieu, Dunstan learned one became good and wise through non-thinking and detachment to anger, hatred, and guilt. Through self-realization hell would become non-existent, killing the existence of all demons, ghosts, and spirits. Here, Dunstan entered the path of liberation. *A glory time coming too!*

The lonely man now glided on a desolate plane, wandering through the shadows of the soul. He attempted to cross this river, where a light emanated. As the world moved on, Dunstan went further, seeing the hell described in scripture, where those who preached and profited from its existence now resided, men imprisoned by their outdated superstitions. As he went further, he saw something even more disturbing. Some souls even had gone so far as to split into two, where a soul of light and a soul of darkness battled for an eternity. *My God! What have they done to deserve this! Such a sight to behold indeed!* Unseen voices and long departed beings begged Dunstan to fall down and beg for forgiveness. *I am no more!*

Dunstan faced a prosecution attorney in a courthouse, where Satan ruled as a judge. They grilled him with questions and accusations, but he did not falter. Suddenly, the forces of nature swallowed him and released him down a never-ending slide into a sea of fire extending for an eternity. *A sight to behold!* There he met the mighty rulers of the world. He saw kings, Emperors, politicians, bankers, media darlings, billionaires, false psychics, presidents, prime ministers, generals, and all their whores, where all wretches burned free of their vices. *Home sweet home!*

All at once, he felt coldness rush up and down his arms and legs. The life-energy of his body contracted. His heart got weaker and his circulation went through a process of slowing down. As his mind got lost in a whirl, he felt the very sensations of sinking into a pool of cold water, almost as if he had begun to dissolve. *The time is coming for me to depart. A given!*

Meanwhile, as his spinal forces went upward, white, blue, and red energy emerged from the heart. In time, Dunstan gradually got pushed into another level of consciousness. Rapidly, he felt his arms and blood being burned by the life streams of fire, yet he felt no pain, but peace. *So very peaceful.*

He sensed his body descending into a milieu equal to that of a boiling point of water. He even suspected the sensation of being pierced by an infinite number of hot needles. A great vibration now ensued. *I feel now I am ready to walk into the light if it ever came.* The life force departed between the eyebrows and many more other parts of the body. As this energy gathered above his heart, he saw a great light shining above his heart. In a skip of a beat, it then flowed downward to the navel. At the navel, a dense mass of fire manifested. *Death a big budget, Hollywood production in itself.*

Dunstan felt his body of energy departing and his body contracting. Something even entered his spine and flowed upwards. The forces traveled through the nerves. It took almost a half an hour to an hour for a multitude of forces to reach the crown of the head, where a great heat of energy had risen and left the body. If only he had not been so overwhelmed with guilty, he would have experienced bliss and none being. Thus, at this moment, Dunstan now found himself overwhelmed by the hallucinations for as yet an unknown period of time. If he only he could forgot about his travels through Hades, which would lead to the inner universe, where immortality would be possible.

At once, he observed a great flash of light that penetrated all matter and energy. He saw the nameless god, in a formless and uncreated state. All the forces of his body now traveled through the many organs and glands, preparing for departure at the crown of the head. Such forces traveled throughout all the chakras. Those moments, atoms and molecules divided, sending out a sonic boom through the skull. *The Manhattan Project all over again*! The eyes flickered open. All the physical life forms of Hades disappeared into the background. He clenched his teeth. When one embarked on the next level of consciousness, one must be at peace with oneself and others.

He penetrated the light of the universe, where billions of galaxies were born and died. Its brilliance unknown, unborn, undying, and uncreated—pure and raw mental energy, where fire and spirit manifested. He saw the forces guide a mass of departing spirits into the next level of consciousness, where men, women, and children of all ages passed through this golden light, becoming one.

However, that moment, as the celebrity drifted deeper into the next level of consciousness, he became overwhelmed with hallucinations. He tried to detach himself from his riches, his desires, fears, and ambitions. In a skip of a beat, he soon learned firsthand that death resembled a mirror. If a man cannot let go of his possessions, his self, and his vices, hallucinations in the afterworld turned evil. These hallucinations tortured him, causing him to yell and scream. When in such pain, his world went dark. *When does it end*?

His image appeared on screen, as if had been the principal actor in a play. He saw his life through Hades from a myriad of directions. He began to detest his egotism, his vanity, and greed. He watched himself break the destiny of his journey that he had already lived. He projected himself back in time; also to those he had relationships. He saw the four courses of possibilities, which interested and eventually horrified him. The actor lost himself in superimposing his world of dreams over his reality, bedeviling himself in a world of illusion.

Dunstan now became aware that he possessed a new body and his other body was now no more. At that time of such a realization, he encountered an ocean of light. He fought to hold onto this level of super consciousness. This spirit tried to hang onto this pure energy, which was the source and return of all souls. *Can't miss this bus*! Meanwhile, at this moment, it passed through this ocean of light, where at some distance the entity saw a giant lake, where a great edifice, shielded the unknown treasure of the underworld. Each successive lake the shadow passed represented a sojourn into the chakras. A lake of diamonds blinded him. *I am near*! He tried to cross this lake. If he did, he would experience bliss and non-being. The celebrity went further and saw a collection of suns, all varying in size and color. Each sun had a path into the white light. They all represented a chakra. He must travel through its highest center and every path to escape this milieu. Dunstan continued to struggle. *This can't go any further! All is lost!* He couldn't let go of his guilt and sense of misgiving. Unwittingly, he had failed at crossing each path and now beheld a grayish lake. In the meantime, as he stood on those dismal shores, he looked toward the horizon, where all his fears, desires, all feelings of guilt and desperation manifested—the sight of his lesser self. Those who wanted to become, or have been. Thus all his desires were realized, which would become a source of agony after judgment.

CHAPTER SEVENTEEN

A blinding light shocked our hero. A myriad of beings manifested, all statuesque, grand, and sublime. Their images chiseled from marble and physical features possessed an awe inspiring glow. Thus, in that moment, Dunstan had failed to overcome the self, inducing such great beings to arise from the oblivion—the judges of heaven and hell. *What do we have here!* Many native tribes believed people don't die, they transform into other animals. This would explain the shape shifting beings that populated the underworld. All of a sudden, in a flash these entities took on the images of a set of Supreme Court justices. *You do the crime, you do the time.* The specters shaped shifted into the shape of alligators, or extraterrestrials. *Who said one bloodline ruled the world?* He failed to overcome the self, inducing a great being to arise from the oblivion—the judges of heaven and hell. They shape shifted into a set of Supreme Court justices and faced the once, famous man.

"Have you seen the evil of your ways?" it cried. "You will never leave this world unless you have redeemed yourself."

All my papers are in order. "Yes I have!" Dunstan countered. "I accept any punishment that you hand out to me!" *A long time coming!*

On the outset, this reaction pleased the court and they beamed at his acknowledgement. "We have spoken," they pronounced. "All will be, will be as if you have not been at all," they proclaimed in unison. The tribunal then disappeared and thus was no more. Our hero saw himself on the road to liberation. Essentially, this lake and this milieu were nothing more than a world of illusion. *When you get there, I'll save you a place.*

As these strange figures vanished into the expanse of time, another image manifested before the repentant soul.

"Who are you?" Dunstan asked. *Who can this be?*

"I am nobody," it replied. *Don't be modest.*

Eventually, Dunstan smiled at the presence of the poet. In this moment of realization, Dunstan understood that good and evil came to be hallucinations superimposed by man. Beyond heaven and hell bliss and non-being came within reach. *Could still be a hidden agenda, but by whom, or what!*

He discerned these hallucinations in the afterworld as an illusion that acted as a temporary escape. In heaven, one could find the saviors and the saints of all the religions. Along with the care free types. Indolent millionaires, musicians that played in old folks bands, and eccentric gardeners all presided here.

If one left Hades, one found him, or herself, on the shores of a quiet, black lake. At its bottom, at that moment, Dunstan discerned a myriad of spirits in a perpetual state of bliss and non-being, free of their attachments and a magnet for those seeking pleasure and solitude. *So close, yet so far away.* If one's mind had been unclouded by thoughts, passion, and possessions, one may enter this surrounding.

In the meantime, he stared into a prenatal care wing of an unknown hospital. *Here again.* Everything was computer coded and robot controlled. He went from pregnant mother to pregnant mother. In time, he unconsciously understood he must choose his birth mother. Whenever he approached a set of expectant mothers, a holographic image gave a brief summary on the unborn child's possible life journey. Some holographic images detailed a quick painful death and others showed a long, mundane life. During this long journey in the underworld, Dunstan knew from Virgil's constant warnings that he must select a birth mother in the next life, or be sentenced to suffer in the shadows of a bodilessness existence. *What a drag that would be.*

Out of the blue, Dunstan felt a gentle vibration and where he saw light colors that illuminated, relaxing his senses. He refused to enter the rooms where he sensed the smell of fire, burned flesh, urine, or excrement abounded. *No thank you!* He also unconsciously avoided the rooms where the light blinded him. The actor even steered clear of a room where he sensed a disproportionate sensation of heat, or cold. Max even avoided the scene where fear and terror had been prevalent. The old actor found an area where the sound of an orchestra played. In the twinkling of an eye, he smelt flowers and heard the singing of campfire songs. *Just like the Michigan Woods.* When his eyes closed, he heard the quick bark of orders and saw the flash of light speed. The men of the future guided him to a new place, free of the restrictions imposed on the underworld. Briefly he meditated on the white light.

The man who had played many parts returned to the chaos of creation, where the individual self could be burned to cinders by a beam of light. In time, he emerged in the sun, where he found peace from the stresses of life.

Periodically, a shaft of light shot from him and fired off into the cosmos above. He felt a vibrating energy that penetrated all shadows and all things. In fact, in a flash, heavy light breathed from a nearby, pulsating sun.

"Reality is a reflection of the universe and the universe is a shifting mirror, reflecting your innermost desires and vices," a voice opined, lustily. *Who could that be?*

Eventually, he saw all his life, the level of realities and the illusion of death as a reflection of moving nothingness. He even faced the void which contained a clear white light. A warm light enveloped him, liberating Dunstan from all the anxieties, anger, and regret. Even his guilt came to be calmed. *Such a feeling! Never want to let it go!* If he did enter the land of peace and non-being, he would cease to be.

"It is mankind's destiny," the guide went on. "It is futile to fight it."

No arguments from me here! You have me here! "I will not fight it!" Dunstan replied, his features solemn with resignation. *You are the boss*!

On this day he left the cave and conquered the self, inheriting the great universe. Immediately, he awoke from the unconsciousness and faced the many gods and demons, the countless Satan's, hells, paradises, and heavens within the cave. They all emerged from the collective unconscious of man. At this stage of the journey, Max understood how he had filled this cave with hallucinations. These images had manifested following the death experiences.

All of a sudden, he saw his corpse appear on a marble table, which levitated from the floor. He saw beams of light firing from the crown of the head and flames of sharp light crawling up its spine. When this strange snake of fire reached the heart, sheets of transcendental force left the heart and engulfed the lifeless body, almost obliterating it before his eyes. *Almost a form of cremation*. When the flame reached the head, its eyes opened.

This image dissolved into a sea of atoms and molecules. In this environ he beheld an uncreated and nameless god in

137

its original form. In a flash, his state of emptiness led him into a sensation of illumination.

"The fires of hell and the demons that occupy it are from the collective unconscious of early man, which was in the evolutionary days of man," the poet said. "Man is destined to evolve and live in the fires of the sun," the great man said. *Who would ever think?*

All his anger, hatred, and guilt burned away. He felt the pains and sorrows of the victims of his pro-gun policy. He saw their faces and that of their families. As this world moved on, he experienced all such sensations in an instant. His self now burned away and he saw god uncreated and in an uncreated form, making him into a realized soul. Somewhere he found the answers where they had been all along. He need not look for them again. Then Mack Dunstan came to be no more. *Ado!*

THE END